Edwin Adams

Notes on the Geology, Mineralogy, and Springs of England and Wales

Edwin Adams

Notes on the Geology, Mineralogy, and Springs of England and Wales

Reprint of the original, first published in 1857.

1st Edition 2023 | ISBN: 978-3-37516-128-6

Salzwasser Verlag is an imprint of Outlook Verlagsgesellschaft mbH.

Verlag (Publisher): Outlook Verlag GmbH, Zeilweg 44, 60439 Frankfurt, Deutschland
Vertretungsberechtigt (Authorized to represent): E. Roepke, Zeilweg 44, 60439 Frankfurt, Deutschland
Druck (Print): Books on Demand GmbH, In de Tarpen 42, 22848 Norderstedt, Deutschland

NOTES

ON THE

GEOLOGY, MINERALOGY, AND SPRINGS

OF

ENGLAND AND WALES.

TO WHICH IS ADDED

A Glossarial Appendix of Names and Terms

USED IN THE WORK.

FOR THE USE OF TEACHERS AND THE UPPER
CLASSES IN SCHOOLS.

BY

EDWIN ADAMS, C.M., T.C.B.,

Master of the Boys' Endowed National School, Dartford, Kent;

AUTHOR OF

"THE GEOGRAPHICAL WORD-EXPOSITOR."

———◆———

LONDON:
LONGMAN, BROWN, GREEN, LONGMANS, AND ROBERTS.
——
1857.

PREFACE.

It must not be supposed that this little attempt is intended as anything more than an initiatory step to a knowledge of the geology of England and Wales. The importance of acquiring some information, however brief, on so useful a subject is so obvious that no apology, it is thought, will be needed for its appearance.

If I should, by this small undertaking, be the means of imparting to a few a thirst for increasing their desire for further instruction on this important topic, my most sanguine hopes will be realized. The young student will find the subject much more ably handled and considerably more exhausted in *Recreations in Physical Geography,* and the *World of Waters,* both by Miss Zornlin (Parker and Son); Page's *Rudiments of Geology* (Chambers); Hughes's *Outlines of Physical Geography* (Longman and Co.); and Reid's *Outlines of Physical Geography* (Oliver and Boyd); in all of which he will discover much that will well repay his perusal. The excellent *Map of the Geology of England and Wales* (National Society), by the Rev.

Samuel Clark, Principal of Battersea Training College, should be studied along with this and other works on the geological formations of this country.

Dexter's *Portable Cabinets of Objects* (National Society) should form part of the furniture of every good school, and especially in such schools where a knowledge of " Common Things " is taught. They are most valuable adjuncts to the usual school apparatus.

Should this endeavour to familiarize the study of British geology meet with a sufficient amount of encouragement, it will shortly be followed by others on the physical geography, history, etc., of England and Wales.

EDWIN ADAMS.

Boys' Endowed National School, Dartford,
January 18th, 1857.

CONTENTS.

NOTES

ON THE

GEOLOGICAL FORMATIONS, MINERALOGY,

AND

SPRINGS OF ENGLAND AND WALES.

———◆———

I.—GEOLOGY.

THE geological formations of England and Wales require very
attentive perusal, and should be studied, as much as possible,
in connection with the physical features of the country. Generally, each particular chain or group of mountains in England
(including Wales) corresponds with a particular formation.
This fact may be exemplified by the following table:—

SYSTEM.	PART OF SYSTEM.	GEOLOGICAL FORMATION.
(1.) PENNINE	Pennine Chain	*Carboniferous Limestone.*
	Cumbrian Group	*Silurian.*
	North York Moors	*Oolitic.*
(2.) DEVONIAN	Mendip Hills	*Cretaceous Formation.*
	North Downs	
	South Downs	
	Chiltern Hills	
	East Anglian Heights	
	Lincoln and York Wolds	
	Essex and Middlesex Heights	*Tertiary.*
	Exmoor	*Carboniferous Limestone.*
	Cornish Heights	*Devonian Limestone.*
	Dartmoor	

SYSTEM.	PART OF SYSTEM.	GEOLOGICAL FORMATION.
(3.)CAMBRIAN	Welsh Mountain generally ..	*Cambrian Formation.* *Silurian, and* *Old Red Sandstone.*

OBSERVATION.—It will appear from this table that the mountain-system of England and Wales may be very conveniently divided into the Pennine, Devonian, and Cambrian.

The highest mountains in Great Britain occur in the Granitic formations. The formations that contain the greatest eminences next to the Igneous (or Granitic) formation are the Cambrian and Silurian; as, Snowdon, 3,571 feet high, in the Cambrian formation; and Sca Fell, 3,166 feet high, in the Silurian (in Cumberland). The next elevations occur in the Old Red Sandstone; as, Brecknock Beacon, 2,862 feet; and in the Carboniferous or Mountain Limestone formation, as, Crossfell, 2,901 feet. Then, in point of elevation, comes the Oolitic; as, Dalehead, 1,862 feet, and Burton Head, 1,485 feet, both in the North York Moors; and Cleveland, 1,134 feet, in the Cotswolds. The Cretaceous or Chalk contains the next heights; as, Inkpen Beacon, between Wilts, Berks, and Hants, 1,011 feet. Next occurs the Tertiary formation; the chief of which are Langdon Hill, in Essex, 620 feet; and Highgate and Hampstead Hills, in Middlesex, both attaining an elevation of about 450 feet. The greatest granitic elevation *in England* is Cawsand Beacon, in the Dartmoor, 1,792 feet.

The formations in England and Wales may be thus classed:

IGNEOUS; including *Granitic* and similar rocks.

PRIMARY; including { *Cambrian* and *Silurian.* *Devonian Limestone.* }

SECONDARY; including
- *Old Red Sandstone.*
- *Carboniferous Limestone.*
- *Magnesian Limestone.*
- *New Red Sandstone.*
- *Oolitic.*
- *Cretaceous.*

TERTIARY; including *Tertiary Formations.*

By *Igneous* rocks are meant those that have for their origin *fire*, or that are, in other words, *of volcanic agency.*

OBSERVATION.—Humboldt, in his " Cosmos," considers rocks under four heads, according to their origin. These are (1.) *rocks of eruption*, called also *igneous, plutonic*, and *unstratified* rocks. Such rocks have issued from the earth either in a fluid or semi-fluid state, at a very high temperature. (2.) *Sedimentary rocks* are such as have been precipitated and deposited on the surface of the earth, from a fluid in which the particles were held in suspension. Sandstone, beds of clay, chalk, &c., may be instanced. (3.) *Metamorphic rocks* are sedimentary rocks, in the formation of which a change has taken place. (4.) *Conglomerate rocks* are coarse or fine grained sandstones or *breccias*—angular fragments cemented together.

———

GRANITIC

are the chief igneous rocks. Granite is composed of felspar, mica, and quartz. The aspect of mountains consisting of granite is extremely diverse. Granite enters very largely into the composition of the European and Asiatic mountains. In England, it occurs in the northern extremity of the mountain limestone formation, in the Cheviot hills; in the western part of the Cambrian group; in several detached portions in Anglesea; and in many places in Cornwall; in fact, granite forms one of the compositions of the Cornish Heights.

OBSERVATION.—If felspar predominate in this rock, the result is a bed of clay: it is durable in proportion as felspar and quartz predominate; and less durable in proportion as mica predominates. The granite used for McAdamizing roads is obtained from Guernsey. Igneous rocks do *not* contain *organic* remains, and are, therefore, *azoic*. When durability in a structure is an object, this rock is had recourse to: buildings composed of granite are the Liverpool and other English Docks, Waterloo Bridge, the Pyramids of Egypt, etc.

THE CAMBRIAN AND SILURIAN FORMATIONS

consist of various kinds of slate. The *Cambrian* is not unfrequently termed the *grauwacke :* its texture differs but little from the clay-slate: it varies in fineness from that of a coarse slate to a conglomerate of pebbles ; and may, with respect to its hardness, be said to be an exceedingly indurated conglomerate. The *Silurian* consists of limestones, sandstones, and shale. The *first fossil* has been found in the rocks of this formation.

Life begins to dawn with the development of the *clay-slate* system : and it appears to become abundant in proportion as the rocks of this system proceed through the Cambrian and Silurian formations. The earliest vital forms are *animals*, though low in the scale : and these are entirely *marine*. The fossils in the clay-state and Cambrian (or grauwacke) systems belong to the species of *zoophytes*, *mollusca*, and *crustacea*. The chief of these are the following: (1.) *Cyathophyllum Cyathus ;* (2.) *Heliopora Porosa ;* (3.) *Catenipora Labyrinthica ;* (4.) *Producta ;* (5.) *Spirifera ;* and (6.) *Terebratula.*

OBSERVATION.—The clay-state formation lies in amongst the Cambrian and Silurian formations.

Encrinites appear for the first time in the Silurian formation. *Marine shell fish* now become more numerous, and, in form, more distinct: such are the *spiriferæ, terebratulæ,* and *productæ.* The *chambered shells* now begin to inhabit the waters. The *trilobite,* the most interesting, and, at the same time, the most numerous type of the crustacea of this period, was a crustacean having eyes of a very complicated nature, and was covered with a shelly kind of plates. Several specimens have been taken of its eye in a not very perfect state: it is said to be formed of four hundred spherical lenses in separate compartments, so disposed that the creature could, in its usual situation at the bottom of the water, readily discern anything around it. This animal (so named from its *three lobes*) is supposed to have travelled through the water by means of paddles, which were too soft to be preserved. The *sirolis,* an animal now living, and of kindred genus with the *trilobite,* is found to have eyes constructed nearly on the same principle.

The *animals* of this period were of two classes:—(1.) those living on *plants,* hence called *herbivorous;* (2.) those living on the *flesh* of others, hence denominated *carnivorous.* Examples of the former were the productæ, the terebratulæ, and others; of the latter, ammonites and trilobites. The ammonite belongs more especially to the Oolitic formation.

The *aspect* of the Cambrian and Silurian formations is bold and mountainous, as is abundantly testified by the Cambrian (or Welsh) and Cumbrian mountains: and Professor Phillips observes, " supported by granite, and mixed with igneous masses, the *slaty* rocks of the English lakes rise to more than 3,000 [in correct words, to 3,166] feet in height, and present a variety of outline and intricacy of combination, which, in connection with clear lakes and considerable waterfalls, leave to Switzerland little superiority."

The *economy* of this system is great and important. Slate, for *writing* purposes, for *roofing* houses, and for *ornamental* uses, is obtained from the clay-slate. Flagstones and pavements are also derived from this formation.

THE DEVONIAN LIMESTONE FORMATION

is frequently termed the OLD RED SANDSTONE FORMATION; the former of these is, however, a more specific appellation. It contains black and veined marble, and calcareous slate.

The *organic remains* are not less interesting than those of the strata above this formation. The fossil plants are, indeed, few and not very distinct; but they much resemble, and are allied to, those of the Silurian formation. The highest division of the animal kingdom, viz., *vertebrata*, is for the first time distinctly traceable. These are *ichthyolites*, or fossil fishes. The chief of the crustacea found in it are the *cephalaspis, pterichthys*, and *coccosteus*. The former (the *cephalaspis*) is overlined with bony plates: the latter has, also, a bony covering, and is supplied with a tail for locomotion. The pterichthys is also enveloped by a bony kind of covering something similar: its peculiar feature is a pair of appendages like wings, which appear not only to have been the means of locomotion, but, moreover, to have served as a kind of defence. It is the best known fossil of the Old Red Sandstone formation. The *cephalaspis, coccosteus,* and *pterichthys* are, most probably, successive advances in the scale of creation, and seem to indicate a higher condition of development than do the organic remains of the Silurian formation; and these former appear to have been less developed than the *holoptychius* and *osteolepis*. The former of these has a bony covering, but it is formed of a larger number of plates, finely enamelled, with the engraving very curious, and its general figure has a nearer approach to figures in existence, having fins and a tail for locomotion. The latter has bony scales which meet one another as the bricks in a house, so that its internal parts are not only protected, but it is thus enabled to bend about in any direction. This animal is so well developed in its structure, that it exhibits fins, a tail, and an elongated form of body, which allow it to put forth a vast deal of strength when required, and to move with great agility.

The Old Red Sandstone formation occurs (to a very great extent in Scotland,) in the south and south-east of Wales, and to a small degree in Anglesea, and has a narrow strip in Somersetshire. The Devonian limestone, so called, occupies almost the whole of Cornwall, and the north and south of Devonshire.

The *aspect* of this formation is not nearly so bold as that of the Silurian, but is much more varied in its general character. Under the name of the Devonian Limestone formation it includes the Exmoor in the north, and the Dartmoor in the south, of Devonshire, and the whole of the Cornish Heights.

—

THE CARBONIFEROUS, or MOUNTAIN LIMESTONE, FORMATION

is probably the most extensive of all the formations, inasmuch as our largest coal-fields are associated therewith. As it is developed in our own country, it may be said to consist of thick-bedded grey or sub-crystalline limestones, separated by partitions of grits and shales; and of whitish quartzose sandstones of various degrees of fineness, divided oy subordinate layers of shale, thin seams of coal, and bands of ironstone. With this formation is also associated *millstone grit*, consisting of a series of very pebbly sandstones. The *organic remains* of the Mountain Limestone are, generally speaking, *marine*. Many beds are entirely composed of the exuviæ of the *crinoid* or *encrinite* family; and masses of limestone have been found of from forty to one hundred and twenty feet in thickness, almost wholly composed of encrinites, thence called *encrinital limestone*. Of the encrinites there were (1.) the *moniliformis*, so called from the necklace form of its neck; (2.) the *pentacrinus*, or five sided instead of round; (3.) the *actinocrinus*, or spiny encrinite; and (4.) the *apiocrinite*, from the pear-like shape of its head.

The Carboniferous formation is geographically distributed over the greater part of the north of England, extending from the Cheviot Hills on the north, to the New Red Sandstone formation on the south, where it is accompanied by the most important coal-fields. It also extends over the greater part of Flintshire, surrounds the Great South Wales coal-field, and exists in several detached portions in Gloucestershire and Somersetshire. A narrow strip of this rock, also, almost entirely encircles the Cumbrian group.

As the most noted *coal-measures* are associated with this system of rocks, this will probably be considered the best place to notice them.

The coal of this country is held in great repute, not only in our own dominions at home and abroad, but also in many foreign countries not subject to our sway: it therefore forms with us a considerable article of commerce. A remarkable sort of coal is called cannel or candle coal, and is found chiefly in Lancashire. In weight it is light; in appearance, glossy;

is liable to split into thin flakes; and, when kindled, gives an excellent blaze until consumed to ashes. Another uncommon kind of coal, found in Staffordshire, and called peacock coal, exhibits the appearance of a peacock's train when turned towards the light. It is not nearly so hard as cannel coal, and will not admit of being polished. Mr. Edward Hughes,* speaking of the coal of Great Britain, makes the following useful remarks:—" It is due to the unrivalled accessibility by sea to the best coal basins of England, Scotland, and Wales, from so many points in the circumference of the island,—where coals of many varieties and admirable qualities can be shipped at the very sites where they are mined—that Great Britain has hitherto been able to furnish such enormous and cheap supplies, not only to the home consumers, but nearly to every maritime country of Europe. In this respect she is far more favourably circumstanced than her rival continental producers—France, Belgium, and Austria, whose coal-fields lie remote from the sea-board.''

Coal-fields are either (1.) *manufacturing*, (2.) *exporting*, or (3.) *home*, or domestic.

The coal-fields, from their geographical position, naturally fall into the following tripartite division: (1.) *the great district in the north;* (2.) *the great district in the centre;* and (3.) *the great district in the west.*

(1.) *The Great Northern District* includes all north of the Trent. The *Northumberland and Durham* coal-field stands first as an *exporting* coal-field. It is traversed by almost the whole of the river Tyne, after its formation by the North and South Tynes. It covers an area of 780 square miles, or 499,200 acres. The chief towns connected with it are Newcastle (which some-

---

* See his excellent *Atlas of Physical Geography* (London: Longmans).

times gives name to the field), North and South Shields, Sunderland, and Durham. London is principally supplied from hence. But this is not the only place to which Newcastle coal is exported; for Scotland, Holland, France, and, indeed, most of the European countries receive coal from here.

The *Whitehaven* coal-field is also *exporting*. Including four detached fields, it covers a space of 150 square miles, or 96,000 acres. Sea-ports connected with it are Whitehaven (hence its name), Maryport, Workington, &c. Vast quantities of IRON are found here. Dublin, and all other seaports on the eastern coast of Ireland, the Isle of Man, and some parts of Scotland, are supplied from this field.

The *Manchester* or *South Lancashire* coal-field contains a great deal of cannel coal. Its principal towns are Manchester (hence its name), Rochdale, Blackburn, Bury, Wigan, Leigh, Oldham, etc. It is connected with the IRON trade; and has an area of about 600 square miles, or 384,000 acres.

The *Leeds and Nottingham* coal-field is one of immense size, occupying a large portion of Yorkshire and Nottinghamshire, and part of Derbyshire. It is bounded on the south by the river Trent, and covers 1,010 square miles, or 646,400 acres. Its chief towns are Leeds, Nottingham (hence its name), Bradford, Huddersfield, Barnsley, Sheffield, and Chesterfield. It lies in an excellent situation with reference to Hull, and is connected with the WOOLLEN trade.

The *Potteries* or *North Staffordshire* coal-field has an area, if we include the *Cheadle* coal-field a little to the east of it, of 78 square miles, or 49,920 acres. Its chief towns are Stoke-upon-Trent, Cheadle, and Bursley; and it is connected with the SILK trade of Cheshire.

(2.) *The Great Central District.* The *Ashby* coal-field lies in the north of Leicestershire, in the neighbourhood of Ashby-de-la-Zouch (hence its name).   Its area is 62½ square miles, or 40,000 acres.   It is not a very important coal-field.

The *Warwick* coal-field lies in the north-east of the county of that name, and encroaches a little into the county of Leicester.   Coventry and Nuneaton are towns sustained by it. It is associated with the SILK trade ; and covers a superficial extent of 60 square miles, or 38,400 acres.

The *Dudley* or *South Staffordshire* coal-field is one of exceeding importance.   Upon it depends the flourishing state of Dudley (hence its name), Birmingham, Walsall, Wolverhampton, Bilston, etc.   Coal is sent hence as far as Reading and Gloucester, although this latter place is very near to another excellent field.   It is excessively rich in IRON, yielding one-third of the whole quantity produced in England.   We should therefore call this an iron-producing coal-field.   Its extent is 1,000 square miles, or 640,000 acres.

The *Coalbrooke-Dale* field, in Shropshire, is traversed by the Severn. One-ninth of the coal produced in England is obtained from this field.   Its chief towns are Coalbrook-Dale (hence its name), Kidderminster, Bridgenorth, Bewdley, and Madely. It is famous for CARPETS ; and covers an area of 60 square miles, or 38,400 acres.

(3.) *The Great Western District,* including the *northern* and *southern.*   In the *northern* division are the *Anglesea, Flintshire,* and *Menai* coal-fields.   In the *southern* are the *South Wales, Dean Forest,* and *Bristol* coal-fields.

The *Anglesea* coal-field lies chiefly in the southern part of the island of that name.   It produces a deal of cannel coal, and its seaport is Beaumaris ; is connected with the COPPER mines ; and covers an area of 18 square miles, or 11,480 acres.

The *Flintshire* coal-measure is the largest in the northern division. Its coal is chiefly cannel, and it extends along the estuary of the Dee and the greater part of the course of that river. Towns connected therewith are Holywell, Wrexham, Parkgate (in Cheshire), and others. It is associated with the CLOTH and GLOVE manufactures; and has a superficial extent of 185 square miles, or 118,400 acres.

The *Great South Wales* coal-field extends through the counties of Glamorgan, Caermarthen, and Pembroke. It is encircled throughout by a narrow belt of Carboniferous Limestone, and covers an area of 1,200 square miles, an extent of surface not attained by any other coal-field in England or Wales. It may be looked upon as the most important in the world. It produces *one-half* of the IRON manufactured in this country. There are twelve beds of coal in this vast measure from three to nine feet in thickness, and eleven more from one and-a-half to three feet in thickness, equal, altogether, to one solid lump ninety-five feet thick. At this rate, there are 60,000,000 of tons in every square mile. The chief towns of this large coal-basin are Monmouth, Merthyr Tydvil, famous for IRON, and Swansea. Cardiff, noted for its manufacture of COPPER, serves the purpose of a seaport to this immense field.

The *Dean Forest* coal-field exists in several detached portions in the county of Gloucester, along the south-west border of the Severn. This field is elevated 900 feet above the sea-level. It is connected with Stroud, and the BROAD CLOTH manufacture. The area of this excellent basin of coal is 45 square miles, or 28,000 acres.

The *Bristol* coal-field also exists in many unconnected spots in Gloucestershire and Somersetshire. Its chief towns are Bristol (hence its name), and Frome; is associated with the manufacture of BROAD CLOTH (though not, by far, so much at the present time as formerly); and may be considered as a *domestic* coal-field. Its superficial extent is 200 square miles, or 128,000 acres.

The coal-measures contain immense numbers of ferns, of which as many as 250 species have been described. As examples, may be mentioned the *Neuropteris, Sphenopteris*, etc. Some of these ferns are evidently *tree ferns*. *Calamites* are the next numerous of the fossil plants found in the coal formation. These bore a great resemblance to the *equisetum*, or horse-tail. The *lepidodendron*, although belonging to the club-moss family, or lycopodiums, attained the size, in very many instances, of a large tree. The remains of *fossil forests* have also been discovered in the coal-fields, as at Parkfield colliery, near Wolverhampton, in which seventy-three trees have been found with the roots connected with the soil in which they grew. This soil now forms a hard rock. In South Wales, also, fossil forests occur one above the other.

Igneous rocks connected with the Mountain Limestone formation are the porphyritic in the Cheviot Hills, the whinsill* of the north of England, and the load-stone in Derbyshire.

Dykes are frequently met with in the coal-fields of the north. The word (comes from the Scottish *dyke, a wall*, or *fence*, and) is applied to those interruptions that the miner often comes in contact with, which *wall off*, as it were, one part of the field from another. These dykes vary in thickness from a few feet to several yards.

---

* *Whinsill* is the local term for the extensive trap formation, which extends from the north of Alnwick to the Tyne, thence along the western side of the Pennine Chain to Brough, and along the Tees to Middleton.

Granitic rocks, connected with the Carboniferous strata, also occur in Anglesea, and very largely in Devonshire.

The next in order to the Carboniferous formation is the

PERMIAN, or MAGNESIAN LIMESTONE, FORMATION.

" *Permian*" is applied to these strata, because these rocks exist largely in *Perm*, a province of Russia.

These strata are not very extensive in England, presenting themselves only in a narrow strip in the counties of Nottingham and York.

Limestone, containing magnesia, is termed *dolomite ;* of this rock the Houses of Parliament are built. The dolomite comes from Bolsover Moor, in Derbyshire. A large deposit, designated *dolomite conglomerate,* or *breccia,* consisting of fragments or pebbles cemented together by dolomite or magnesian limestone, abounds very largely at Durdham Downs, near Bristol. The dolomite breccia contains fossil remains of reptiles, among which may be mentioned the *thecodonto-saurus* and the *palæo-saurus.* Dolomite received its name from M. Dolomien, a French naturalist of the last century, who died in the first year of the present century. He is stated to have visited the several volcanoes of Italy, after which he was sent, accompanied by other men of science, to collect and give a description of all the antiquities and natural curiosities of Egypt. His death took place after he had visited Mont Simplon, whence he returned wealthy in mineralogical acquisitions.

The Magnesian Limestone strata contain the fossil remains

of *toads* and *frogs* which were as large as bulls: they are called *batrachian* reptiles ; from a word signifying *frog-like.*

Lying next are the

NEW RED SANDSTONE

strata, which, in Germany, have received the name of *Trias,* or *Triple ;* because, in some parts of that country, three distinct formations are referred to by it. These are the *banter,* the *muschelkalk,* and the *keuper.*

This formation lies over a great extent of England ; occupying the chief of the Midland counties, the whole of Cheshire, great part of Yorkshire, also a portion of Cumberland, Devonshire, etc. *Rock-salt* is found in the valley of the Weaver. It is found particularly at the " wiches," as Northwich, etc.

OBSERVATION.—The termination " *wich* " in Cheshire *appears* to have some connection with *salt ;* as does *hall* on the continent.

The composition of the New Red Sandstone strata may be said to be *arenaceous, argillaceous, calcareous,* and *saline.*

It is worthy of note that, with the exception of the South Wales and Dean Forest measures, all the coal-fields *border* on this formation.

This rock looks nice as a building-stone, of which the finest specimen is Hereford Cathedral. It is, however, not so valuable a stone as, upon inspection, one might be led to suppose. Like the Magnesian strata (sometimes included in the New Red Sandstone), this formation contains the *batrachian* or *frog-like* animals. The fossil reptiles of this period afford much interest to the geologist. The species of reptiles that have been discovered much resemble toads and frogs, thence called batrachian: and the name *labyrinthodon* has been applied to them, from the *labyrinth-like*, or complicated, structure of their teeth. Because the fossil reptiles were first known by their *hand*, the appellation *cheirotherium* was also bestowed upon them.

The *aspect* of this formation is not by any means bold, as may be inferred from the total absence of granitic rocks in connection with them.

THE OOLITIC FORMATION

is of great importance, consisting of several beds of various kinds of useful limestones, of clays, sand, and gravel (including WEALDEN). These strata occupy a large portion of the country, and correspond with the North York Moors (their northern extremity) and the Cotswold Hills : from the Cotswolds they extend to Lyme Regis, in Dorsetshire (their southern extremity). By the *Wealden* is implied that district lying between those two lines of chalk, the North and South Downs.

The three divisions of this formation are (1.) the *lower* oolite; (2.) the *middle* oolite; and (3.) the *upper* oolite.

The *lower* oolite includes (*a.*) the *inferior oolite*, or strata of calcareous freestone and yellow sandstone, met with in the Cotswold Hills, and Dundry Hill; (*b.*) beds of *fuller's earth*, near Bath; (*c.*) the *great Bath oolite*, at Bath; (*d.*) *Stonesfield slate*, at Stonesfield, near Woodstock, extending thence to Scarborough, Whitby, and Tees mouth; and (*e.*) the *cornbrash* and *forest marble*, occurring in Wiltshire.

The *middle* oolite comprises (*a.*) *Oxford clay* (so called from its existence in the county of that name), a dark-blue kind of clay; and (*b.*) *coral rag*, a calcareous freestone, containing a number of corals (found in the same locality).

The *upper* oolite comprehends (*a.*) a bituminous shale, an imperfect kind of earthy coal, called *Kimmeridge clay*, from a place of that name in Dorsetshire; and (*b.*) *Portland stone*, and *sand*. Portland stone is obtained chiefly from the island of Portland, in Dorsetshire; and is the material of which St. Paul's Cathedral and several other noble structures are composed.

The *organic remains* of this formation are exceedingly numerous and important. They indicate a decided advance in the scale; and several new tribes of vegetables are added to the already existing flora. The *flora* and *fauna* may be thus enumerated :—

(1.) Of *plants—sea-weeds; equisetums;* several *ferns; cycadæ; coniferæ; lilacæ;* etc.

(2.) Of *animals—zoophytes; crinodia; star-fish; echinida,* or *sea-urchins; shell-fish; annulosa; crustacea; insects* resembling the *beetle* and *dragon fly; fishes,* chiefly belonging to the *ganoidia; reptiles;* and *mammalia.*

Most characteristic of the Oolitic formation are the *echini; ammonites;* the *lizard* or *sauroid reptiles;* the *ptero-dactyles;* and the *marsupial mammalia.* The word *echinus,* or sea-urchin, is the zoological term for *sea-hedgehog.* The *ammonite* was a chambered shell belonging to the *cephalopodous* division of the mollusca; and its name was derived from Jupiter *Ammon,* to the horn on the head of which it bore a striking resemblance. It is one of the most numerous of the widely-diffused mollusca of the secondary strata, and has been discovered to be of various sizes, from that of a pin's head to three or four feet in diameter.

The *sauroid* (or *lizard*) animals have been thus classed, according to their means of locomotion :—(*a.*) *swimmers*, or those having paddles; as the *ichthyosaurus* and *plesiosaurus* ; (*b.*) *those with limbs like mammalia*, fitted for terrestrial life ; as the *megalosaurus* and the *iguanodon ;* and (*c.*) *those analogous to living amphibia ;* as the *protosaurus, geosaurus*, etc.

The chief of these are the *itchthyosauri* and *plesiosauri* of the Oolitic, and the *iguanodon* of the Wealden, formation.

The *ichthyosauri* (or *fish-lizards*) were aquatics provided with paddles, their great characteristic. They are proved to have been carnivorous animals, not only from their jaws and teeth, but also from the circumstance of the remains of fish and reptiles having frequently been found in their skeletons. They often attained a great size; and a skeleton found at Lyme Regis appears to have belonged to an animal not less than twenty-four feet in length. The general form of this reptile was, as appears from its skeleton, something similar to the crocodile; having, however, instead of feet, feet by which it was endowed with locomotion.

The *plesiosaurus* (or *near neighbour*) was peculiar in the shape of its neck, which was of an extraordinary length, measuring nearly half the extent of the animal. Its head, in proportion, is small; and its tail, short, stout, and pointed. The vertebræ of its neck exceed, in number, those of any other animal known. Both the ichthyosaurus and its *near neighbour*, the plesiosaurus, were occupants of the water, and must have moved with great difficulty on land. The latter is conjectured to have had frequent need of respiration, as it breathed air ; and, in order to effect this, it generally, it is supposed, kept near the surface, arched back its neck like a swan, and plunged it downwards into the water at the fishes that came within its reach.

The *iguanodon*, the characteristic of the Wealden, is supposed to have been an herbivorous animal—that is, one adapted to live on the herbs of the field, or on vegetable substances. This conjecture has arisen from the peculiar structure of its teeth. It was furnished with a horn on its nose, and its length was from ninety feet and downwards.

The *aspect* of the Oolitic formation is tame compared with that of the lower strata : it is, nevertheless, pleasing.

The *economy* is important. In it is found *fuller's earth*, more especially in Wiltshire (near Bradford) and in Surrey. *Portland stone* is obtained, as we have seen, from the island of the same name in Dorsetshire.

Next above the Oolitic is the

CRETACEOUS FORMATION.

It occupies an extensive tract, and coincides with the greater part of the mountain system in England. In the north it terminates (at Flamborough Head) in a high cliff; on the south side of the Wash, it commences again at Hunstanton Cliff and Cromer, and extends thence into Dorsetshire. In Wiltshire, it diverges into two branches eastwardly, one corresponding with the North, the other with the South, Downs. It is the best defined of all the geological formations.

The *organic remains* of this formation are eminently *marine*.

The few *plants* which are found are *algæ, confervæ*, and *seaweeds of marine types*. Of the *animal* remains, the following are found in abundance : *sponges* (if these belong to the animal kingdom), *corals, star-fish, annulosa, mollusca, crustacea, fishes*, and *reptiles*. But with one exception, mammalia are not known.

The remains of the *iguanodon* have been found in the rock, termed *Kentish rag*, near Maidstone, in Kent.

The Chalk or Cretaceous formation has been divided into three kinds of strata: (1.) *chalk marl;* (2.) *pure white chalk;* and (3.) *chalk with flint.*

The *aspect* of the chalk districts is smooth, the hills gently flowing into valleys which, in their turn, gradually ascend and form, generally, rounded hill-tops.

Next above the Cretaceous strata is the

TERTIARY FORMATION.

Originally (that is, before the times of Cuvier and Brogniart), this was not regarded as a distinct formation, but as mere superficial accumulations that could not be referred to any distinct period. Generally speaking, these strata are loosely aggregated, and are not of very great thickness. This formation differs from that next below it in three distinct particulars: (1.) in its mineral composition; (2.) in the higher order of organisation that it contains; and (3.) in its superficial sands and clays.

The Tertiary formation is divided into (*a.*) *eocene;* (*b.*) *meiocene;* and (*c.*) *pleiocene.*

The *eocene* have been further classed into five groups:—(1.) *plastic clay;* (2.) *London clay;* (3.) *Bagshot sands;* (4.) *Barton beds;* and (5.) *freshwater beds.*

The word *eocene* (as, indeed, were also the two other terms) was given by Sir Charles Lyell, and is applied to those strata which contain very few of the fossil shells of the Tertiary system. It is of Greek origin, and comes from *eos,*=*the dawn,* and *kainos,*=*recent.*

London clay contains many organic remains. Of the fossil *flora* are some species of *cocoa nuts*; and of the genus *nipidates*. Several seeds have also been found; viz., of the *laburnum*; *accacia*, or *mimosa*; *custard apple*; *cucumber*, etc. Belonging to the *testacea* are the *nautilus*; *voluta*; *cerithium*, etc. *Turtles*; *crocodiles*; *serpents*, etc., have also been discovered; as also the remains of a bird of the *vulture kind.*

The *Barton beds* are also rich in organic remains, which consist of shells, of which 209 species have been found in the cliffs of the same name.

The *freshwater* (or *fluviatile*) beds in the north of the Isle of Wight, and at Hordwell Cliff, in Hants, possess many fossil remains, the most remarkable of which are the *anoplotherium*; *palæotherium*; *chæroptamus*; and the *dichobune*. All these are accompanied by bones of *crocodiles*; *tortoises*; and *snakes*. The remains of a carnivorous animal have also been found at Hordwell Cliff, called the *hyænodon.*

The *meiocene* are probably absent in our own country; but they exist in France and other countries on the continent. The word *meiocene* comes from the Greek *meion*, $=$ *less*, and *kainos*, $=$ *recent*; and is applied to those strata which contain *less* than half of the *recent* fossil shells of the Tertiary System.

The *pleiocene* strata are subdivided into two groups:—(1.) the *pleiocene*, sometimes called the *older pleiocene*; and (2.) the *pleistocene*, sometimes designated the *newer pleiocene*. *Pleiocene* comes from the Greek *pleion*, $=$ *more*, and *kaínos*, $=$ *recent*; and is applied to those strata which contain the *more recent* of the fossil shells of the Tertiary System. *Pleistocene* signifies *most recent*; and is a term bestowed upon the *most recent* fossil shells of the Tertiary formation. It comes from the Greek *pleiston*, $=$ *most*, and *kainos.*

Many fossils are met with in these strata, more particularly in that portion of them called the *pleistocene.*   At Brentford, in a freshwater deposit, have been discovered the bones of an extinct species of elephant, called the *mammoth,* and likewise of the *rhinoceros,* of which latter, a great number have been found. Associated with these are the remains of the *hippopotamus;* a *short-horned ox; red deer; rein deer; lion,* or *tiger;* and *monkey.* At Gray's Thurrock, in Essex, is a similar deposit containing bones of other species of *elephants, rhinoceroses,* etc.   Near Hasborough, in Norfolk, a submerged forest exists, containing so large a number of the bones of elephants, that it received the name of *elephant bed.*   At Cromer, in Norfolk, the fossil remains of a *gigantic beaver; ox; horse; deer; and rhinoceros* have been found.

II.—MINERAL PRODUCTIONS.

———

THESE are many and important. The chief of them (besides *coal*, already spoken of) are *iron; tin; copper; lead; salt; zinc,* etc.

Iron is very generally scattered; and it is an important and valuable fact that their geographical locality is nearly or entirely coincident with that of the several coal basins. It would be very difficult of access were it not for their ready and immediate connection with these basins. Prior to the year 1713, iron was manufactured and worked by means of charcoal, and not mineral coal. In the reign of James I., there were 400 furnaces in Sussex, Surrey, and Kent, which were supplied with fuel obtained from the Forest of Andreade. At the same time, there were, in Wales, 200, and, in Nottinghamshire, 40 furnaces; making a total of 640. Since this period, our coal and iron trades have increased to such a degree, that it is estimated that one-half of the coal, and two-thirds of the iron, produced in the whole world, are obtained from the mines of Great Britain, which, in 1850, amounted to two and-a-half millions of tons of iron, and forty millions of tons of coal.

The chief iron-producing districts for coal are the South Wales coal-field, which yielded in 1850, 700,000 tons; the Dudley coal-field, 600,000 tons; and the Coalbrook-Dale field.

The former of these is, in this respect, the most important in the world; its chief town for the manufacture of iron, especially that for railroads, is Merthyr Tydvil, in the north of the coal-measure. Staffordshire contains some very important iron works, comprising a district of 50,000 acres.

It must not, however, be considered that this useful mineral is only found in the districts just mentioned; for it exists in several localities where it yields a great abundance. The chief of these are in the (1.) Whitehaven, (2.) Northumberland, (3.) Leeds and Nottingham, (4.) Potteries, (5.) Flint, and (6.) the Dean Forest coal-field.

Tin is a metal of a silver-white colour, the chief properties of which are malleability and ductility. It has been known from the earliest times, and was, probably, in common use in the time of Moses. The Egyptians employed it in the arts, and the Greeks used it as an alloy. It was sometimes spoken of under the name of *white lead*, and is used by Pliny. It early formed an article of commerce with our ancestors; for the Phœnicians were in the habit of procuring it from this country. Aristotle asserts that the tin mines of Cornwall were known and worked in his days; and Diodorus Siculus describes the method in which the mines of this metal were worked. Our tin mines are chiefly situated in Cornwall and Devonshire, but more particularly in the former county. They appear to have been neglected under the Saxons; but their successors, the Normans, under the direction of the Earls of Cornwall, paid great attention to them. Edward the Third confirmed privileges that had been bestowed upon the tinners, and converted Cornwall into a dukedom, with which he put his son Edward the Black Prince in possession; and, since that time, the heirs apparent to the English Crown have enjoyed it successively. The Cornish tin mines are placed under certain regulations known by the name of the Stannary Laws. The number of these mines exceeds one hundred thousand.

Copper is of a pale red color, tinted with yellow. The chief locality for this metal is, like that for tin, Cornwall. In this country we do not find its wealth on the surface, but in the interior. While the agriculture on the surface affords employment to only a few, the rich interior furnishes occupation to 60,000 people. Copper has not been worked in this country nearly so long as tin, probably in consequence of its position, which is further from the surface than that metal. In fact, it was not worked with any spirit till about a century back. From 1726 to 1735 the mines yielded, on an average, about 700 tons annually of pure copper; from 1776 to 1785 the annual production amounted to not less than 2,650 tons. In the year 1798 it was more than 5,000 tons; and it now reaches more than double that amount, being worth, at £100 per ton, £1,200,000 sterling. The famous copper mines at Parys Mountain, near Amlwch, in Anglesea, were discovered in 1768, when its prodigious productions were astonishing: since that year they have, however, greatly declined. Besides Cornwall and Anglesea, copper is found in small quantities in Durham, Yorkshire, Cumberland, Staffordshire, and Devonshire.

Lead is raised in very large quantities in Cumberland, Northumberland, Somersetshire, Devonshire, Cornwall, Denbighshire, and in great abundance in Wales. The lead which is raised in England and Wales contains about eight ounces of silver; and, owing to improvements in the processes, it is found to be of advantage to extract it. In this way, silver, to the value of £30,000, is produced.

Plumbago, graphite, or black lead, is found in immense quantities in but one mine in England: this is situated at Borrowdale, near Keswick, in Cumberland. It is made use of in making pencils; in forming composition for crucibles; and in covering the outside of iron utensils to preserve them from rust, to give them a good appearance, and to lessen the friction of machinery. When this mine was first discovered has not been ascertained; and, till recently, it was only worked at intervals. It does not exist in veins, but in irregularly shaped masses; and these are not always good, being frequently hard and gritty: when, however, a soft mass is discovered it is worth several guineas a pound. The best is sent to London, where dealers may obtain it once a month. The proprietors of the article will not allow any to be disposed of until it has been deposited in their own warehouse: the pencil makers at Keswick, therefore, receive their supplies from the metropolis. The color of the metal is a dark iron-black, and its chief characteristic is that of possessing a kind of slaty fracture. It will probably be remembered that it is found in the slate formation.

III.—SPRINGS.

SPRINGS are occasioned by rain penetrating the earth till its progress is arrested by strata the particles of which are placed more closely in contact with each other: here it forms cavities of water or subterraneous reservoirs at various depths which, when full, generally force a passage through the ground either *above* or *laterally.*

The first great division of springs is into *hot,* or *thermal;* and *cold.* They are, again, either *natural* or *artificial.*

Mineral Waters are divided into seven' great classes. These are (1.) *acidulous* or *carbonated;* (2.) *chalybeate* or *ferruginous;* (3.) *sulphureous;* (4.) *saline,* which are either (*a.*) *brine,* or (*b.*) *medicinal;* (5.) *calcareous;* (6.) *siliceous;* and *bituminous* or *petroleum.*

OBSERVATION.—Springs, in any case, contain a certain proportion of air and gas, and some solid matter generally in the form of salts. When the solid contents do not exceed a three-thousandth part of the whole, the springs in which they are contained are termed *soft-water* springs. When the solid contents exceed this proportion, such springs are called *hard-water* springs. If springs are charged with solid matter in great abundance, they are known as *mineral waters.*

(1.) The appearance of *acidulous* or *carbonated* springs is sparkling, occasioned by the presence of carbonic gas which has the property of decomposing the very hardest rocks with which it happens to come in contact, particularly those (granite, for instance,) that contain felspar. Their chief characteristics are their acid taste, and their disengagement from fixed air. Instances of this kind occur at *Tunbridge Wells*, in our own country ; and at *Pyrmont* and *Seltzer*.

OBSERVATION.—Carbonic acid gas was evolved from a well near the Epsom race-course at the depth of 200 feet; and from another at Norbury Park, 400 feet in depth. At Bexley Heath it rushed out, putting out all the workmen's candles, and attended with fatal results. It should not, however, be supposed that, although deleterious in its free state, this gas is injurious in water. Water, as is the case with the Seltzer waters, when saturated by this gas, has a very sparkling appearance when poured from one vessel into another. When this gas exists in springs in large proportions, the water bubbles up as if boiling. The most remarkable of this description occurs in Asia Minor, known by the appellation of the *Fountain of Asbamæus;* and, from accounts that have reached us, it may be inferred that it has, for 1600 years, exhibited precisely the same phenomena that it does at the present day.

(2.) *Chalybeate* or *ferruginous* springs are those which are charged with oxyde of iron, usually combined with various salts ; and some of these contain carbonic acid, and thus combine themselves with acidulous springs. Such kind of spring is termed an *acidulated chalybeate* spring, an instance of which occurs at *Tunbridge Wells.* Of this first kind may be instanced one at *Wick*, near Brighton.

(3.) By *sulphureous* springs are meant such as contain sulphur, which is met with in the form of sulphuretted hydrogen, or that of sulphate of lime. The springs of this class, in our own country, owe their quality to sulphuretted hydrogen. Such are the springs of *Harrowgate,* etc.

OBSERVATION 1.—What has been asserted of acidulous, may also be affirmed of sulphureous, springs. We saw that the Fountain of Asbamæus had, in all probability, existed for 1600 years in the same condition : in like manner, hot springs are now in *Bithynia,* in Asia

Minor, which, according to the description given of them by Greek writers, must have been similarly constituted some 2000 years since as they are at the present time.

OBSERVATION 2.—The largest of the *Baden* springs, near Vienna, is *Haupt-quelle*, or *High-well*, of this class, which yields 40,950 cubic feet of water daily; depositing, at the same time, sulphate of lime.

(4.) *Saline* springs are of two kinds: (*a.*) *brine*, and (*b.*) *medicinal salt* springs.

(*a.*) *Brine* springs contain, more or less, chloride of sodium, or common salt, which is of vast importance to man. It is sometimes found that water from these springs contains one quarter its weight in salt; this is, however, very rare. The saline properties appear to be derived from the subterranean masses of salt through which the brine springs pass. These latter are found in the greatest quantities in the New Red Sandstone formation, more especially in that part of it in the neighbourhood of the " wiches," as Droitwich, Nantwich, Middlewich, etc.

(*b.*) *Medicinal salt* springs are those charged with a considerable proportion of neutral salts, or sulphate of soda, carbonate of soda, sulphate of magnesia, etc., which impart to the waters a disagreeable taste. These they contain in addition to chloride of sodium or common salt. The *Cheltenham* waters may be cited as an example. The chief ingredients of these waters are chloride of sodium, sulphate of magnesia, and sulphate of soda, which, including other constituents, are derived from the red marl in which these waters have their origin.

OBSERVATION.—The red marl belongs to the New Red Sandstone formation, the grand repository of rock salt.

(5.) *Calcareous* springs are such as are highly charged with calcareous matter, and occur in the limestone rocks. They are frequently met with, and present phenomena of vast interest. While the deposition of calcareous matter is going on, it often happens that plants and other substances near the spot become encrusted with, and sometimes embedded in, the *tafa* or *tavertin*, thus apparently converted into stone, in which state they may be permanently preserved: in such case, the springs are generally called *petrifying* or *mineralizing* springs.

OBSERVATION.—*Petrifying* springs are to be seen in several parts of the country; but these, in point of grandeur, are not to be compared with those of other countries. One of our most celebrated is the *Dropping Well*, at Knaresborough, in Yorkshire. It has its rise at the foot of a limestone rock, on the south-west side of the river Nidd, opposite the ruins of the Knaresborough Castle. After running about twenty yards towards the Nidd, it spreads itself over the surface of a cliff; it then trickles down a number of places, dropping very fast, and making a kind of tinkling sound in its fall. It sends forth about twenty gallons of water per minute; and, while it goes on in a rapid motion, the fine particles existing in it in great abundance are slightly deposited: but, as it makes an approach to the cliff, it meets with a gentle ascent, its pace becomes languid, and a petrifying substance, which is extremely beautiful, is deposited on twigs, grass, stones, and, in fact, on any projection. Small branches of trees become encrusted with spar, and form a very interesting spectacle.

On the continent are dropping wells (1.) at *Sandarrah*, in the Himalaya Mountains; (2.) at the hill of *San Vignone*, in Tuscany; (3.) the celebrated baths of *San Filippo*, not far from San Vignone; and (4.) the *Rio San Pedro*, remarkable for the lapidifying powers of its waters.

(6.) *Siliceous* springs are those that hold silica, or flint, in solution. They do not occur nearly so frequently as calcareous springs. Water will not hold silica in solution unless the liquid is raised to a very high temperature, and therefore these

waters are arranged under the head of *thermal* springs. When
the water of these springs comes in contact with the air it is
rendered cool, and thus the property of holding silica in solution is annihilated. The most celebrated instances of this
class of springs are the *Valley das Furnas*, and the *Geysers*.

OBSERVATION.—The *Great Geyser*, in Iceland, has its rise in a large
basin situated in the midst of a small mound formed by the deposits of
the spring. The jets from this fountain rise to various heights, as ten
feet, thirty feet, ninety feet, etc. It has been stated that they sometimes
rise to the height of two hundred feet. Petrifactions are here met with,
and look extremely beautiful. Leaves of birch and willow are sometimes seen, which have been converted into white stone in a perfect
state of preservation, every fibre being quite entire. The temperature
of these fountains is somewhat above the boiling point.

(7.) *Bituminous* or *petroleum* springs are impregnated with
petroleum and the several minerals bearing relation to it, as
naphtha, asphaltum, bitumen, etc. These springs are of common occurrence in volcanic regions, or in those parts in which
traces of igneous action are observable. Such are the districts
bordering on the Caspian Sea, etc. These springs are not,
however, confined to volcanic and such-like districts, as may
be seen in the Artesian well lately formed in the Bas Rhin
province, where a jet of water has been obtained largely
impregnated with petroleum.

By *thermal* or *hot* springs are meant those the temperature
of which is above that of the locality in which they occur.
As an instance, we may cite the mineral and thermal spring
at *Bakewell*, in Derbyshire, the temperature of which is 62°
Fahrenheit, while that of the surrounding country is but
49° Fahr.; if, however, the same spring could be placed in
Sicily, still having the same degree of heat, it would not then
constitute a thermal spring, as the mean temperature of that

country is 63° Fahr. This rule is, nevertheless, subject to some modification. Among the most remarkable of this description of springs are the *Geysers*, of Iceland. The *Great Geyser*, at the depth of eighty feet, has been found to have a temperature of 257° Fahr., which is 45° above the boiling point: and the *Small Geyser*, at the depth of fifty feet, has a temperature of 232° Fahr., or 20° above the same point. In a small hole at the surface of the ground water has been found to have a temperature of 214°. Others remarkable for their high degree of heat are in the island of St. Michael; in Hungary; the mineral springs of the *Rhine provinces;* and the springs of Central France, especially those of *Mont D'Or.*

A GLOSSARIAL APPENDIX.*

A

Algæ. One of the seven natural tribes into which the vegetable kingdom is distributed. All the sea-weeds and many other aquatic plants are included under this title.

Ammonites, or Snake-stones, are spiral fossil shells, found in great abundance in the chalk and oolite formations. They appear like a snake rolled up. Two hundred and forty species have already been described.

Anoplotherium. An extinct genus of quadrupeds, nearly allied to the pachydermata. It is found in a fossil state in the freshwater beds of the Isle of Wight.

Animal. From the Latin *anima*, = *life*. An animal is defined to be "a living body endued with sensation and spontaneous motion." In its general application, "animal" is used to denote an irrational creature, as opposed to man, the only rational being. Linnæus, the great naturalist, says animals *live, grow*, and *feel;* vegetables, *live*, and *grow;* while minerals only *grow*. It is, however, often difficult, and, in many cases, impossible, to draw the line.

---

* In this Appendix, the letters *G. W. E.*, after the exposition of a geographical name, refer to the Author's *Geographical Word-Expositor*, where a fuller explanation of the several names may be sought. (London: Longmans.)

ANGLESEA signifies the *island* of the *Angles*, or *English*, who became possessors of this *island* in the reign of Edward I., when he conquered Wales. The Anglo-Saxon *ea*, or *ey*, = *an island*, or *land near water*. The root is by some, and not without a great degree of probability, supposed to be the Latin *aqua*, whence the French words *eaux*, *Ouse*, etc. *G.W.E.*

ANTIQUITY. From the Latin *antiquus*, = *old*, or *ancient*.

ARENACEOUS signifies *sandy ;* from the Latin *arena*, = *sand*. Rocks that are rather loose in texture and moderately fine have this term applied to them.

ARGILLACEOUS rocks are those composed entirely of *clay*, or in which *clay* is the principal constituent. The Latin *argilla* = *clay*.

ASPECT. The *aspect* of a country implies its *appearance*, from the Latin *ad*, = *to*, and *specio*, = *to see*.

AUSTRIA is, in German, called *Oesterreich*, or the *eastern kingdom ;* and was so entitled in reference to the Emperor Charlemagne's dominions, of which *Austria* occupied the *easternmost* portion. *G.W.E.*

AZOIC rocks are such as do *not* contain *organic* remains. Igneous rocks are *azoic*. *Azoic* is derived from the Greek *a*, = *not*, and *zoe*, = *life*.

B.

BAGSHOT SANDS (The) consist principally of siliceous or flinty sand, and occupy a very large tract of country around Bagshot (in Surrey), and in the New Forest (Hants). A *serpent* has been discovered in the Bagshot Sands at Bracklesham Bay, 20 feet in length. The Bagshot Sands belong to the *Eocene* period.

BARTON BEDS (The), around Barton, are composed chiefly of a marine deposit, which is exceedingly rich in *fossil shells*, of which as many as 219 species have been discovered in the Barton Beds. They, like the Bagshot Sands, are of the *Eocene* period.

BATRACHIAN signifies pertaining to *frogs;* and is applied to an order of reptiles including frogs, toads, and other animals allied to them.

BELGIUM. A name obtained from the ancient inhabitants of the country, who were called *Belgæ*. By the Romans it was termed *Gallica Belgica.* The Belgæ were one of the three nations into which Cæsar divided the inhabitants of Gaul, or France: hence its name as *Gallica Belgica.* *G.W.E.*

BIRMINGHAM is the principal hardware manufacturing town in England. It is probably but an altered form of *Bermicham*, the ancient appellation of the town, so called from a family of that name who possessed the manor. *G.W.E.*

BRISTOL. Was called, by the Britons, *Caer Oder nant Baden,* = the *city of Oder in Baden* (or *Bath*) valley; and, also, *Caer Brito;* and, in Anglo-Saxon, *Brightstowe*, or the *pleasant stow*, or *place*, which is easily corrupted into *Bristow* and *Bristol.* *G.W.E.*

BRITAIN signifies the *painted* nation; from *bryth*, or *brith*, = *tinted, variegated*, and *painted.* *G.W.E.*

BRECCIA, sometimes called PUDDING-STONE, is a kind of aggregate earth, consisting of broken particles of stone united by some common cement.

C.

CALAMITE. So called from the reed-like jottings of its stalk. It was anciently used as a pen to write on parchment or *papyrus.*

CALCAREOUS. Applied to rocks, etc., that contain a very large proportion of *lime;* from the Latin *calx,* = *lime.*

CARBONIFEROUS. Applied to rocks that contain, or that are associated with, *coal.* It is derived from the Latin *carbo,* = *coal,* or *charcoal,* and *fero,* = *to carry,* or *bear.*

CARDIFF. From the Celtic *cathair* (and that from the Latin root *castra*), = *an encampment,* and *Taaf,* the river on which Cardiff stands. *G.W.E.*

CAMBRIAN. Pertaining to *Cambria,* the ancient name of Wales.

CARNIVOROUS. A term applied to the fifth order of quadrupeds, or beasts of prey; or, in other words, those that live on *flesh;* from the Latin *caro* (carnis), = *flesh,* and *voro,* = *I devour.*

CANNEL-COAL. The *Bitumen ampelites* of Linnæus. It burns with a very bright flame, like a *candle.* It is often made into trinkets, as it is capable of being cut and polished.

CEPHALASPIS. Covered with bony plates, and takes its name from the *buckler-shape* of its *head;* from the Greek *kephale,* = *the head,* and *aspis,* = *a buckler.*

CHAIN. Given to the elevations of the earth's surface, to islands, lakes, etc., when their length by far exceeds their breadth. Thus, we say, the " Pennine *Chain;*" the " *Chain* of the Andes;"etc. *G.W.E.*

CHILTERN HILLS (The) derive their name from their *chalky* nature and composition; *cealt, cylt, chilt,* in Anglo-Saxon, meaning *chalk.* *G.W.E.*

CHEIROTHERIUM. Derived from *cheir,* = *the hand,* from the *hand-like* impressions of its feet.

CIRCUMFERENCE. From the Latin *circum,* = *round,* and *fero,* = *to bear,* or *carry.*

COCCOSTEUS. Enveloped in a *bony* covering, furnished with

a tail for locomotion, and the name is derived from the Greek *kokkos*, = *a berry*, and *osteon*, = *a bone*.

COMPOSITION. From the Latin *con*, = *with*, or *together*, and *pono*, = *to place*.

COAL is a solid inflammable substance, of a bituminous nature, used largely for fuel.

CONGLOMERATE ROCKS are angular fragments cemented *together* into a *ball;* from *con*, = *together*, and *glomus* (*glomeris*), = *a ball*, or *clue*.

CONIFERÆ. *Cone-shaped flowers*, as the juniper, fir, etc. They are the fifty-first natural order of plants, according to Linnæus. *Coniferous* is a term hence applied to all trees bearing *cones*.

COPPER. One of the six primitive metals, the color of which is pale red, tinged with yellow. The Latin for *copper* is *cuprum*.

CORAL RAG is a calcareous freestone which contains a number of *corals*. It belongs to the Middle Oolite.

CORNBRASH probably derives its name from the ease with which it disintegrates and yields to the plough, being (according to the provincial term) *brashy* enough (or able to be *broken*) to prepare the ground where it exists for the growth of *corn* or any other kind of grain.

CORNWALL. From the British word *cernyw*, = *a horn*, and *walli*, = *foreign*. *G.W.E.*

COTSWOLDS is the designation applied to a tract of high land in Gloucestershire, in consequence of the sheep-*cots*, which were, at an early period, formed on these *hills*, or *wolds*. *G.W.E.*

CRETACEOUS ROCKS are such as contain a very large proportion of *chalk;* from the Latin *creta*, = *chalk*.

CROCODILE. A large and fierce animal of the genus *Lacerta*.

It is amphibious, and inhabits the large rivers of Asia and Africa.

CRINOIDEANS. An extinct class of invertebrate animals. See ENCRINITE.

CRUSTACEA. Fish covered with *shells;* as crabs, lobsters, etc.

CUMBRIAN. Pertaining to *Cumbria* (or *Cumberland*), the land of the *Cymri.*

D.

DARTMOOR. A district in Devonshire which contains the source of the *Dart.* The Anglo-Saxon *mor,* = *a moor,* or *heath.* *G.W.E.*

DEPOSIT. Any matter which has settled down from water. Deposits are (1.) river, or fluviatile; (2.) lake, or lacustrine; (3.) sea, or marine; and (4.) sea-shore, or littoral. The word is from the Latin *de,* = *down,* and *positus,* = *placed.*

DERBYSHIRE. *Derby* is a contraction of *Derwenthy;* or the Anglo-Saxon *by,* or *dwelling,* on the *Derwent.* *G.W.E.*

DOLOMITE. A variety of magnesian carbonate of lime, so named after the celebrated French geologist, *M. Dolomieu.*

DOWNS. From the Celtic word *dun,* = *a hill.* *G.W.E.*

DUBLIN. From the Celtic *dubh,* = *black,* and *lyn,* or *lin,* = *a pool,* or *deep pool.* *G.W.E.*

DURHAM. The *ham,* or *home, of wild animals;* from the Anglo-Saxon *deor,* = *a wild animal.* Durham was also called *Dunholm,* from the Celtic *dun,* = *a hill,* and *holm,* = *an island;* it being on an eminence surrounded almost entirely by the river Wear. The bishop signs himself *Dunelm.* *G.W.E.*

DYKES. See page 13.

E.

ECHINUS. This is the generic name for *Sea-urchins*, or *Sea-eggs*. The *Echinodermata* are a class of invertebrate animals, all inhabitants of the sea. The *Echinus vulgaris*, so often found in a *fossil* state, cannot now be traced among those *living*.

ENCRINITES (or *Stone Lilies* as they are commonly called) are a genus of *petrified* radiated animals, deriving the name from the Greek *krinè,* = *a lily.* There are many genera and sub-genera of the encrinite, of which the *encrinites moniliformis* may be taken as the type of the class. Other important branches of the class were the *pentacrinus* (*five-sided* instead of round), the *antinicrinus* (or *spiny*) and the *apiocrinite* (so called from the *pear-like* form of its head).

ENCRINITAL LIMESTONE is *limestone* almost wholly composed of *encrinites.* This, when hard, is a highly ornamental marble.

EGYPT. *Aia Koptou* was the name bestowed upon the country by the Greeks; this was afterwards contracted into *Aikoptos,* which was more subsequently softened into *Aiguptos,* or *Ægyptus,* which = the *land of the Copts.* Abridged from *G.W.E.*

EMINENCE. Applied to elevations on the earth's surface. It is from the Latin *emineo,* = *to excel.*

ENGLAND. Derived from *Engle,* = *the Angles,* and *land ;* meaning, therefore, the *land* of the *Angles,* an important tribe of the Saxons who conquered Britain. The Dutch form of *England* is *Engeland ;* the German orthography is the same as our own. The French *Angleterre* is the nearest approximation to the original form and sound. *G.W.E.*

EOCENE. A term given by Sir Charles Lyell to those strata

of the Tertiary Formation which indicate where the *dawn* or commencement of *recent* animals takes place. *Eocene* comes from the Greek *eos*, = *the dawn*, and *kainos*, = *recent*.

EQUISETUM. In botany, *Horsetail.* A genus of plant in the Linnæan system. Natural order of ferns.

ERUPTION, ROCKS OF, are such as have issued from the earth, either in a fluid or semi-fluid state, at a very high temperature. They are also known as *igneous, plutonic, unstratified, Neptunian,* or *volcanic* rocks.

ESSEX = the country of the *East Saxons*, which formerly included, besides the modern county of Essex, part of Herts. *G.W.E.*

EXMOOR = the *moor*, or *heath* (from the Anglo-Saxon *mor*, = *a heath*), containing the source of the *Exe.* *G.W.E.*

EXUVIÆ. The Latin for *cast clothes.* Applied, in geology, to fossil remains of any description. (It has a different application in zoology.)

F.

FELSPAR, sometimes called *Feldspar*, is a mineral compound of silica, potash, and alumina. It is one of the constituents of granite; softer than quartz, harder than glass, and usually of a white, reddish, or greyish color.

FERNS. Weeds of the *cryptogamia* class. They are very common in dry and barren places, and are exceedingly injurious to the land where they take root. In the torrid zone, several species form small trees, looking something like palms, and are considered great ornaments in those regions.

FAUNA are *animals* peculiar to a certain region, district, or country.

FLORA. *Flowers* and plants peculiar to a certain region, district, or country.

Flamborough Head. So called from its *lighthouse*, set up as a guide to mariners; or from the *fires* that used to be kindled on the cliffs here, which are 500 feet high. *G.W.E.*

Formations. The common name for the various strata of which the crust of the earth is composed; and which are thought to have been formed at different remote dates. In most of the formations there are some mineral or fossil affinities characteristic of the system to which they belong.

Fossil. Any substance mixed up with earthy or metallic particles, which has been *dug* out of the earth. A *fossil* is literally that which is *dug* up; from the Latin *fossus*, = *dug*. Fossils are either *native*, or *extraneous*; *native* are earths, salts, and metallic bodies; *extraneous*, bodies of vegetable or animal origin, as plants, bones, shells, etc., many of which are petrified.

Fossil Forests. See page 13.

Fluid (from the Latin *fluo*, = to *flow*) is a term applied to all bodies, the particles of which easily yield to any amount of pressure.

Fragment. A *broken* part, from the Latin *frango*, = to *break*.

France was conquered by the *Franks*, a people who came from *Franconia*, one of the oldest circles of Germany. *G.W.E.*

Freshwater Beds. See page 21.

G.

Geology is the science which investigates the composition of the crust of the earth, and is derived from the Greek *ge*, = *the earth*, and *logos*, = *a discourse*.

Ganoidia. Fishes of this order are enveloped with angular scales, internally composed of bone, and coated with enamel, from the bright surface of which (enamel) the *ganoid* order of fishes received its name; the Greek *ganos* meaning *splendor.*

GLAMORGANSHIRE derived its name from *Gwlad Morgan* (that is, the *county* of *Morgan*), who was a prince of South Wales. *G.W.E.*

GLOUCESTER is either derived from the British *glow*, = *beautiful*, or from the Welsh *gleaw*, = *strong*, and *castra*, = *an encampment*, or *fortified place*. The Saxons called it *Gleaucestre. G.W.E.*

GRANITE. A rock composed of crystals of felspar, mica, and quartz, and is of igneous origin. Its color is generally greyish; but, from the oxide of iron contained in the felspar, it is sometimes reddish.

GROUP. A term used as opposed to *chain.*

GRAUWACKE signifies *gray rock*, and is a term used by German miners, applied to those greyish slates and siliceous conglomerates, which English geologists designate *Cambrian*, or *Silurian.*

H.

HERBIVOROUS. A term given to those animals that feed on *herbs;* from the Latin *voro*, = *to devour.*

HILL. Any eminence attaining the elevation of 999 feet, or under. All heights beyond this are called *mountains.*

HOLLAND. A European country, implying *hollow* or *low land*, the greater part of the country being *below* the level of the sea. It is derived from the German *hohl*, = *hollow. G.W.E.*

HOLYWELL. Derived its appellation from *St. Winifred's*

Well in its vicinity, to which miraculous powers were formerly attributed. *G.W.E.*

HOLOPTYCHIUS. A fossil fish of the Old Red Sandstone formation, so termed from the *wrinkled* surface of its large enamelled scales; from the Greek *holos*, = *whole*, or *entire*, and *ptyche*, = *a wrinkle*.

I.

ICHTHYOLITE. Any *fish*, or part of one, found in a fossil state, is termed an *icthyolite;* from the Greek *ichthys*, = *a fish*, and *lithos*, = *a stone*.

ICHTHYOSAURUS. A genus of extinct marine animals which united the characters of the *sauroid* (or *lizard*) reptiles, and *fishes;* from the Greek *ichthys*, = *a fish*, and *saurus*, = *a lizard*.

IGNEOUS. A term applied to unstratified rocks that had their origin in *fire*.

IGUANODON (The) is an extinct gigantic reptile, the remains of which were discovered by the famous geologist, Dr. Mantell, in the Wealden formation, and in the localities of Maidstone, Purbeck, and the Isle of Wight.

IRELAND. The native name of *Ireland* is *Erin*, or *Ierne*. *Hibernia*, the name by which, according to Strabo, the country was known to the Romans, is derived from *hiver*, = *winter*, because they imagined it to be a cold and dreary country. *G.W.E.*

IRON (in Latin, *ferrum*), one of the hardest, most useful, and most widely-distributed of the metals. It is found associated with the Carboniferous Formation.

ITALY. Some early writers derive *Italia* from *Italus*, a chieftain of the Œnotri; while others deduce it from the

Greek *italos*, $=$ *an ox*, from the number of fine *oxen* which the country produced. But the Roman historian, Niebuhr, says that *Italia* means nothing more nor less than *the country of the Itali.*   *G.W.E.*

K.

Kent.   From the British or Celtic word *can*, or *ceann*, which $=$ *a head*, or *projection*.   *G.W.E.*

Kentish rag.   Rocks of chalky limestone, in Kent.

Kimmeridge clay consists of dark laminated clays, with gypsum and bituminous shale.

L.

Labyrinthodon.   See page 16.

Lancaster signifies the *encampment*, or *fortified place*, on the *Lune*.   *G.W.E.*

Leicester $=$ the *encampment*, or *fortified place*, on the *Leir* (the ancient name of the Soar).

Lepidodendron.   So named from the *scaly* exterior of its *bark;* from the Greek *lepis*, $=$ *a scale*, and *dendron*, $=$ *a tree.*

Lilac.   A beautiful shrub or plant of the genus *Syringa.*

Lincoln was called by the Romans, *Lindum Colonia;* from the Celtic *lyn*, $=$ *a deep pool*, *dinas*, $=$ *a hill*, and the Latin *Colonia*, $=$ *a colony;* thus meaning *the colony on the hill near the water* (of the Witham).   *G.W.E.*

London.   Either from *lyn*, or *lin*, $=$ *a deep pool*, and *dinas*, $=$ *a hill;* or from *lhong*, $=$ *ships*, and *dun*, or *thun*, which is equivalent to the Saxon word *town;* thus meaning the *town of ships*, for there is every reason to believe that the spot was greatly frequented by vessels in consequence of the excellence of its position. *G.W.E.*

LONDON CLAY. Rocks belonging to the eocene group.

LOCOMOTION = *motion* from *place* to *place*; from the Latin *locus*, = *a place*, and *moveo*, = *to move*.

M.

M'ADAMIZING. A mode of making roads first made known to the public by Mr. M'Adam. The method consists in breaking the stones so small that they may bind with the earth into one smooth and solid mass.

MAMMOTH. An extinct species of elephant, discovered in a fossil state; but wholly distinct from the existing species of either Asia or Africa. Adams, a traveller in Siberia, found the skeleton of a mammoth nine and a half feet high, and fourteen long. The tusks were nine feet in length.

MAIDSTONE = the *town* on the river *Medway*, in Kent. *G.W.E.*

MANUFACTURE. Anything formed from the raw materials, or productions of a country into a state suitable for use; as cloths from wool, etc. Literally, to *manufacture* an article is to *make* it with the *hand*; from the Latin *manus*, = *the hand*, and *facio*, = *to do*, or *to make*.

MAMMALS. In zoology, that division of animals which suckle their young; from *mamma*, = *the breast*.

MAGNESIAN LIMESTONE is carbonate of lime associated with carbonate of magnesia. The extent of country over which it is distributed is not accurately ascertained, as yet.

MEIOCENE. A term given by Sir Charles Lyell to those rocks that show the commencement of *less recent* animals; from the Greek *meion*, = *less*, and *kainos*, = *recent*.

METAMORPHIC ROCKS are such as have undergone, or are undergoing, certain metamorphoses, or *changes of shape*, in their sedimentary character; from the Greek *meta*, = *change*, and *morphe*, = *shape*, or *form*.

MIMOSA (The), or *Sensitive Plant*, received its name from its remarkable property of receding from the touch; thus exhibiting signs, as it were, of animal life and *sensation*.

MICA. One of the constituents of granite, consisting of numerous thin laminæ adhering to each other. It is a mineral of a foliated structure; and is often indiscriminately called *Muscovy glass*, *glimmer*, or *talc*.

MINERALOGY is the science which teaches us the nature and properties of *minerals*, and to classify them according to their characteristics.

MIDDLESEX = the county of the *Middle Saxons*. Abridged from *G.W.E.*

MOLLUSCA. A term given to a class of animals, the bodies of which are *soft*, wanting in an internal skeleton, or articulated covering; from the Latin *mollis*, = *soft*.

MONILIFORMIS signifies having *one shape*, *form*, or *figure*; from *monos*, = *alone*, and *forma*, = *shape* or *form*.

MONMOUTH stands at the confluence of the rivers *Munnow* and Wye. *G.W.E.*

MOOR is derived from the Anglo-Saxon word *mor*, = *a heath*.

MOUNTAIN. See HILL.

N.

NAUTILUS. A genus of marine animals, the shell of which is formed of one continuous piece.

NEUROPTERA. One of the orders into which the class *Insecta* is divided. They are distinguished by having four wings, each pair being membraneous and transparent, reticulated with veins ; as the dragon fly, the lion ant, etc.

NEWCASTLE took its name from a *castle* erected here by Robert, son of William the Winner, as a check upon the inroads of the Scots. *G. W. E.*

NEW RED SANDSTONE FORMATION (The) is called, by some geologists, *Poikilitic*, from the Greek *poikilos*, = *variegated;* and *Saliferous*, or *salt-yielding*, or *salt-bearing*.

NORTHUMBERLAND signifies *land north* of the *Humber;* and, though its application is so restricted now, the name was originally applied to the Anglo-Saxon kingdom which extended from the *Humber* on the south, to the Forth on the north. *G. W. E.*

NOTTINGHAM is contracted from *Snotenga-ham*, the ancient name of the town, probably from *snotenga*, = *caves*, and *ham*, = *a home*. *G. W. E.*

NUNEATON. A market-*town* in Warwickshire which derived its appellation from a *convent* of Benedictine monks that was situated here. *G. W. E.*

O.

OOLITE. Derived from the Greek *oon*, = *an egg*, and *lithos*, = *a stone;* so named from the similarity many of the beds bear to the roe or *eggs* of a fish.

ORGANIC applied to animal or vegetable structures, because made up of parts admirably adapted to each other ; from the Greek *organon*, = *an instrument.*

OSTEOLEPIS (The), which presents the form of a perfect fish, derives its name from the Greek *osteon*, = *a bone*, and *lepis*, = *a scale*, from its *bony scales.*

OXFORD CLAY. Dark-blue clays, with subordinate clayey limestones and bituminous shale.

P.

PALÆOSAURUS. Derived from *palaios*, = *ancient*, and *saurus*, = *a lizard*.

PALÆOTHERIUM. A genus of extinct pachydermatous quadrupeds. *Palæotherium* comes from the Greek *palaios*, = *ancient*, and *therion*, = *a wild beast*. It was discovered along with the *anoplotherium*.

PENNINE. From the Anglo-Saxon *beann*, which means *a hill, mountain*, or *promontory*. *G. W. E.*

PENTACRINUS. A genus of *Radiata*, most specimens of which are found in a fossil state. The stalk of the pentacrinus is *five-sided* (hence its name) instead of round. They are sometimes called *five-angled lily-shaped animals*.

PERMIAN. See page 14.

PLASTIC. This term is applied to lower beds in the Tertiary strata from the fact of the clay readily receiving any impression made by the potter; from the Greek *plasso*, = *to form*.

PLEIOCENE. A term applied by Sir Charles Lyell to strata that contain the fossil remains of *more recent* animals; from the Greek *pleion*, = *more*, and *kainos*, = *recent*.

PLEISTOCENE. Those rocks which contain the *most recent* fossil remains of animals, or those which approach more nearly to existing orders. *Pleiston* (Greek) = *most*, and *kainos*, = *recent*.

PLESIOSAURUS. The name of a genus of extinct marine *Saurians* or *lizards* of very gigantic dimensions. It is distinguished by its great length of neck, small head, and short body and tail.

PLUMBAGO, also called *graphite*, and *black lead*, is a mineral composed of carbon and iron.

PLUTONIC ROCKS. See ERUPTION, ROCKS OF. *Plutonic* is a term diametrically opposed—as applied to rocks—to *Neptunian*. The *Plutonists* attribute the formation of the world in its present state to *igneous* action; but the *Neptunists* maintain that it has a *watery* origin.

PORPHYRY is a granular and crystalized mass, the composition and colors of which are various. It is very hard, and susceptible of a very fine polish.

PORTLAND STONE. A compact kind of sand-stone found in the island of Portland, in Dorsetshire. It consists of a coarse grit cemented together by an earthy spar.

PRIMARY ROCKS are such as are considered to be the oldest, or earliest formed, containing fossils.

PTERICHTHYS. A fossil genus of fish discovered in the Old Red Sandstone. Its characteristic is a pair of *wing-like* appendages, which appear to have aided it in locomotion, and to have acted as a sort of defence when attacked. Hence its name; which comes from the Greek *pteron,* = *a wing*, and *ichthys,* = *a fish*.

PTERODACTYL. A genus of extinct fossil reptiles, which, from their structure, are supposed to have occupied that place in the economy of nature now assigned to *bats* and *insectivorous birds*. It derives its name from the Greek *pteron,* = *a wing*, and *dactylos,* = *a finger*.

Q.

QUARTZ is a kind of siliceous (or flinty) stones, of various colors. It is one of the constituents of granite, and is abundantly circulated throughout the globe.

F

R.

REPTILES. A name applied to all creeping animals, or such as rest on one part of their body while the other portion of the body is advancing or receding.

RUSSIA is said to have derived its name from the *Ruotzi*, or *Rutzi*, which = *foreigners*, or *adventurers*; and is an epithet which the Finns applied to the slavonic occupiers of the aboriginal territory. *G.W.E.*

S.

SALINE. Pertaining to, or containing, *salt*; from the Latin *sal*, = *salt*.

SCOTLAND. So named from the Scots, a people of Ireland who invaded the northern division of the island in the first half of the sixth century, A.D., and who, by degrees, became the sole possessors of the country. *G.W.E.*

SEA-WEEDS. See ALGÆ.

SECONDARY ROCKS are those strata that are placed over the *primary* or transition masses.

SEDIMENTARY ROCKS. Such as have been deposited on the earth's surface from a fluid in which the particles were held in solution. The word is derived from the Latin *sedere*, = to *sit*, or *settle down*.

SHELL-FISH. See ECHINUS.

SAUROIDS, or the *lizard* family, are usually classed according to their organs of locomotion: these are (1.) SWIMMERS, or those fitted with paddles, as the *ichthyosaurus, plesiosaurus, mesosaurus*, etc.; (2.) THOSE WITH LIMBS LIKE MAMMALIA, and adapted for terrestrial life, or the *iguanodon*, and *megalosaurus*; and (3.) THOSE ANALOGOUS TO LIVING

Amphibia, as the *geosaurus, protosaurus, plesiosaurus, hylæosaurus,* etc.   The word is derived from the Greek *saurus,* = *a lizard.*

Shale.   A kind of shist, or slate clay, generally of a bluish or yellowish grey color; but sometimes greenish or blackish. It very commonly bears vegetable impressions.

Silurian.   Applied to a geological formation first of all by Sir R. I. Murchison, which consists of those argillaceous and calcareous beds that lie between the grauwacke and old red sandstone systems.   These rocks are very clearly developed in that part of Wales anciently occupied by the *Silures;* hence their name.

Species.   This epithet is applied to a collection of organized beings of the same common parentage, of the same peculiar form, and liable to change from the influence of circumstances only within certain narrow limits.

Sponge.   Naturalists do not yet seem decided whether to place sponge in the animal or the vegetable kingdom, some referring it to the animal kingdom, while others contend for its vegetable nature.   It was originally thought to be merely a marine fungus, adhering to rocks, etc.; but it has been subsequently classed as a genus of the *Vermes Zoophyta.*

Star-fish, or Sea-star.   A genus of animals that feed on oysters, that belong to the class *vermes,* and to the order *mollusca.*

Stafford.   From the Anglo-Saxon *staef,* = *a staff,* and *ford* (from the Anglo-Saxon *faran,* = *to go*).

Springs are *natural* fountains of water, which have their origin in some reservoir or sheets of water stored beneath the surface of the ground.   Springs are (1.) mineral, including (*a.*) *acidulous,* (*b.*) *chalybeate,* (*c.*) *sulphureous,* (*d.*) *saline,* (*e.*) *calcareous,* and (*f.*) *siliceous* springs.   *Saline* springs are of two kinds, (*a.*) *brine*, and (*b.*) *medicinal salt* springs. (2.) THERMAL, or HOT springs, which may be arranged into two divisions, viz., (*a.*) those which owe their high temperature to the natural heat of the earth at certain depths; and (*b.*) those which owe it to volcanic action. These latter are usually distinguished as *bituminous*, or *petroleum* springs.

STONESFIELD SLATE. Flaggy grits and oolites, found at *Stonesfield*, near Woodstock, in Oxfordshire; and extending thence to Scarborough, in Yorkshire.

STRATA, plural (*Stratum*, singular), is a term given to rocks that lie in succession upon each other. One layer of rock is called a *stratum;* from the Latin *stratus*, = *strewn*, or *spread out.* Rocks thus arranged are said to be *stratified;* and those that present no appearance of having, as it were, been *spread out* are called *unstratified.*

SURREY means the *south kingdom;* from the Anglo-Saxon *suth*, = *south*, and *rica*, = *a kingdom.* Some, however, make it to have reference to its position with regard to the Thames; *ea*, Anglo-Saxon, meaning *an island near water.* *G.W.E.*

SWITZERLAND signifies the *land* of the *Schwitzers*, or *Swiss.* *G.W.E.*

T.

TERTIARY. Under this epithet are included all those regular strata of marl, clay, limestone, sand, and gravel, which occur above the chalk formation. They frequently embrace vast quantities of organic remains of the larger animals.

TESTACEA. A division of the class *vermes*, and of the order *mollusca.* Of this order there are thirty-six genera.

TEXTURE. From the Latin *texo*, = *to weave.*

THECODONTO-SAURUS signifies the *sheath-toothed saurian*, or *lizard*.

TOADSTONE. A dark-brown basaltic amygdaloid, consisting of basalt and green earth, and containing oblong cavities having calcareous spars.

TRIASSIC ROCKS are those that contain fossils more' or less allied to oolite types. They are so called from their being divisible into *three* groups, viz., the Bunter Sandstein, Muschelkalk, and Keuper Marls.

TRILOBITES, so named from their *three lobes*, are crustaceans that form a connecting link between the *Phyllopoda* and the *Pecilopoda*.

U.

UNSTRATIFIED ROCKS. See ERUPTION, ROCKS OF.

V.

VERTEBRATA. *Vertebral animals* are red-blooded, with brains and a spinal chord; *invertebral animals*, on the contrary, have white blood, no skull, and no back bone.

VOLUTA. A genus of univalve shells; as the admiral shells, tiger shells, etc.

W.

WALES = *foreign country*. Abridged from *G.W.E.*

WARWICK = *war town*. Abridged from *G.W.E.*

WEALDEN. So named from the *wealds, wolds, wilds,* or *woods,* of Kent and Sussex, where the deposit thus named prevails.

" WICH." See page 15.

WHINSILL. See page 13 *note*.

Y.

YORK. Called, in Anglo-Saxon, *Eurewic*, i.e., the *wic*, *vicus*, or *dwelling-place*, on the Yorkshire Ouse, anciently called the *Ure*. *York* is a contraction of *Eurewic*. The Romans called it *Eboracum*, and the archbishop signs himself *Ebor*. *G.W.E.*

THE END.

OPINIONS OF THE PRESS

ON

ADAMS'S

GEOGRAPHICAL WORD-EXPOSITOR.*

"*The Geographical Word-Expositor* contains correct explanations of geographical terms and names of places."—*Athenæum.*

"An interesting and instructive department of etymology is elucidated in *The Geographical Word-Expositor* by Mr. Adams..........*The Geographical Word-Expositor*, under an intelligent master, may be made a most useful and interesting class-book for students, combining the study of etymology and history with that of geography."—*Literary Gazette.*

"Of *The Geographical Word-Expositor* by Mr. Adams we formerly expressed a favourable opinion, as being an instructive and interesting class-book. In the second edition the work is much extended and rendered still more worthy of recommendation..........In a volume of one hundred and fifty pages, only a selection of places can be given, and Mr. Adams has, as far as possible, introduced what may be called representative words, making his manual a key-book to geographical nomenclature. An appendix contains lists of roots, prefixes, affixes, and other materials out of which geographical names have been commonly constructed. Tables of cognate equivalents and of geographical synonyms further increase the usefulness of the book for the purposes of tuition or reference."—*Second Review of the Literary Gazette.*

"This little work has required long study by an assiduous collector of information. The intention is apparent from the title. Mr. Adams proposes to explain the meaning of the names attached to places......In addition to the meaning of names, the Author gives a short description of the places..........We like the design of Mr. Adams's little book."—*Tait's Edinburgh Magazine.*

"This is a useful little educational work, on a good plan, well carried out..........That this is really a *desideratum*—or rather *was* such—must be evident to every one who has heard of the recent civil service examina-

*London : Longmans, Second Edition (price 2s. 6d.)

tions, at which the most ordinary geographical questions received no answer, or worse than none, even from men or boys who met other parts of the examination with credit. Mr. Adams's object has been to fix a knowledge of important places in the memory, by giving the etymology of their names, and thus to lay a foundation for further knowledge: and we hope that the work will be put to a fair trial in the large schools. Mr. Adams has done well in applying this method to geography, and we would suggest to him to do the same for history, at least in one of its branches, in as portable and unpretending a form."—*Monthly Review of Literature, Science, and Art.*

" The very useful *Geographical Word-Expositor* of Mr. Adams has promptly reached the second edition."—*Second Review of the Spectator*.

" *The Geographical Word-Expositor* is a new and very useful aid to the study of geography and topography. It is a sort of small dictionary of terms found in geographical books, familiarly and clearly explaining their meanings."—*Critic.*

" A very valuable school-book, the object of which is to give the scholar the derivations of the larger proportion of those names which he meets with in the course of his geographical studies. It may even be profitably consulted by more advanced students."—*Second Review of the Critic.*

" A most useful little addition to the educational library......It is sure to be welcome."—*Eclectic Review.*

" *The Geographical Word-Expositor.*—Under this title the Author, who is himself practically acquainted with the art of teaching, has given a series of explanations, simple and concise, of geographical names and terms used in geographical science. The little book is well adapted for its object, that of rendering the study of geography less mechanical and less dry."—*John Bull.*

" On the first appearance of this little work we expressed our opinion of its usefulness, and we are pleased to see this opinion confirmed by the fact of a second edition having been called for within the space of a few months. The notion upon which it was founded was an original one, and it was to be expected, therefore, that, on the first attempt to carry it into practical effect being ushered into the world, suggestions would reach the Author from various quarters. Of these he has availed himself in the present edition, for the purpose of making his book more complete and more generally useful."—*Second Review of John Bull.*

" The etymology of places' names is correctly given in this clever little work."—*Second Review of the English Journal of Education.*

" The Author of this invaluable treatise merits the thanks of students of geography for supplying them with so concise and intelligible an exposition of geographical nomenclatures. It is a miscellany of useful knowledge, the importance of which we cannot too highly extol, and too strenuously recommend. To pupil-teachers and the upper classes in schools it is a rich gift; a gift which has won the approving testimony of no less a man than Dr. Latham, who remarks that the meaning of a certain word is not all the student derives; he is also introduced to many other points of knowledge. And, furthermore, that the exposition of geographical names does more to make a map a source of pleasure than can be done by any other mode of teaching. Commended by such a voice of authority, it is hardly necessary, nay, it is almost presumptuous, for us to add a single word respecting its merits. We will only observe that the Author has shown great industry in the compilation. Wide and discursive has been the range which he proposed to himself when he commenced his *Word-Expositor*, for not only had he to traverse the terraqueous globe for materials, but also to penetrate the meaning of words, and search in various languages for the origin and root whence they were derived, and then to analyse and simplify them for the use of students; supplying, at the same time, a succinct historical account of each name.

"The book is entitled to general recognition, and merits the patronage of all teachers and students of the science of geography."—*Literarium, or Educational Gazette*.

"We rejoice to see this attractive and very useful little volume making its 'second appearance' under such favourable circumstances, and with so many approving voices proclaiming its merits, and bespeaking another and, if possible, still kinder, welcome for it. It cannot but be gratifying to us to see the *Word-Expositor* coming forth improved both in spirit and in form; growing in favour as it grows in age, and 'winning golden opinions' from every section of the press, as well as from teachers; for we had the privilege of being among the early few who became sponsorial sureties for it, and who had commended its many peculiar features and rare sources of information. We find now, to our great gratification, that the pledge we ventured to give for its excellence has been more than redeemed.

"The *Word-Expositor* has transcended our highest expectations, and has far increased the estimate we had formed of its merits. It is a source of no ordinary pride and pleasure to us to find that our opinion, pronounced almost at the first introduction of the book to public notice, should be echoed by almost the united voices of the press, and approved by the ablest teachers in the kingdom. Nor are we indifferent to the honour done us by the publishers, in assigning to us so distinguished a place in the great muster-roll of the press. They have placed us in the front ranks of this great civilizing army; and we have no doubt that a large supplemental corps will soon be added, which shall spread still farther the fame of the *Word-Expositor*, until it shall become 'familiar as a household word' in the school and the college.

"We need not repeat in this place our opinion respecting the advantages which the *Word-Expositor* confers on teachers and pupils. It is already on record, and is ratified by a thousand voices. It only remains for us to add that the Author has shown himself deserving of the praise bestowed upon him, by the energy and care with which he has revised and improved the second edition. Instead of reposing on the laurels he had won, and contenting himself with the measure of success he had already obtained, he girds himself afresh like a grateful and generous worker, and makes another round of the earth, looking with curious eye upon all its varied features and distinctions, and pausing here and there to make fresh *reconnaissance*, in order that he might present the reader with a more complete key to the knowledge of geographical nomenclatures. He was also mindful to carry with him on his tour some of the ablest and most approved guides as a further means of aiding him in his pursuit of knowledge and enabling him to test and prove the accuracy of his own observations. He has by this course fully shown the earnestness of the spirit with which he entered on his work, his zeal as a scholar, and his desire to earn some additional title to the reward so handsomely conferred upon him by the press and t:achers of England.

"We are also glad to perceive that the Author has, in the present edition, marked the correct pronunciation of the most difficult names belonging to geography. In our opinion, next to the knowledge of a name is the knowledge of the manner in which it ought to be pronounced; for defective pronunciation would mar the finest oration of Cicero or Demosthenes. It sensibly detracts from the merit of any kind of composition, and in public estimation lowers the standard of a man's abilities and attainments, however learned he might otherwise be……….Entertaining such sentiments as these, we could not but approve the Author's judgment in making the important addition of pronunciation to his valuable work, a work which has our best wishes for its continued prosperity as it has our unaltered opinion of its merits and great importance and utility to teachers and pupils. It is a book which should be in every school and library. It will occupy only a small space in either; but it contains within its thin covers vast stores of information, gleaned from every part of the terraqueous globe, and many niceties of origin, and derivations of names of mountains, rivers, islands, cities, lakes, oceans, and continents, which belong exclusively to it, and which will be looked for in vain elsewhere."—*Second Review of the Literarium, or Educational Gazette.*

"This little volume will be found well calculated to awaken a greater interest in geography, and to impress more deeply on the memory the names of places mentioned in the daily lessons."—*Notes and Queries.*

"It is a little work which will add interest to the study of geography."—*Papers for the Schoolmaster.*

"We are glad to find that the *Word-Expositor* is favourably received, thus early presenting itself in a second edition, very considerably enlarged and greatly improved………Mr. Adams is unknown to us, except through his book, but we feel interested in his effort."—*Second Review of Papers for the Schoolmaster.*

"Hitherto, the student of geography, when he has wanted to know the meaning and derivation of a geographical name, has, in most cases, had to look over several works and at last to find his search too often end in disappointment. But now even pupil-teachers will be able to provide themselves with a work which will assist them greatly in these studies. Mr. Adams has evidently bestowed great labour on the little book before us, and we are sure that his work will be found to be of great use in conjunction with our ordinary geographical text-books."—*School and the Teacher.*

"We felt ourselves bound to speak in terms of warm commendation of the first edition of this work: it contained so much excellence that we expected no long time would elapse before the public would demand another edition, but we did not expect to see in the second edition so great an improvement on the first. Many new names are added; fuller particulars are given in many instances; while an entirely new feature has been introduced in the pronunciation of the most difficult names. No school, no schoolmaster, we would even say, no pupil-teacher should be without this work, which, once known, will be in constant requisition both in the school-room and in the study."—*Second Review of the School and the Teacher*.

"*A Geographical Word-Expositor* is very much needed in our school literature. Mr. Adams's little book is a praiseworthy attempt to supply this *desideratum*. We duly appreciate the laconic form of derivation given in such words as ' Acton,' in Middlesex, from the Anglo-Saxon *ac*, *an oak*, and *ton*, *a town*………The contents are valuable, and indispensable to every one who would wish to understand our geographical nomenclature."—*British Educator*.

" The object is proper and useful; the execution, good; the arrangement, simple; the list, extensive."—*Scottish Educational Journal*.

" This book meets a want which all teachers must have felt, as it furnishes information which could only be obtained by considerable research. In reference to etymology, a great diversity of opinion obtains; but Mr. Adams has evidently bestowed on his work great care, and he will be found a safe guide."—*Educator*.

" This plan Mr. Adams has very successfully executed; and there are few adults, however learned, who will not find it useful to have such a manual on their table. The definitions are full, and, as far as we can judge, etymologically correct………A little cheap volume like this, crowded with information, does supply a *desideratum*."—*Clerical Journal*.

" Will be found a useful manual for schools, and, indeed, for a large class of adults."—*English Churchman*.

" This is a useful little portable volume………The design appears to have been ably carried out. Students of geography will owe a considerable debt of gratitude to Mr. Adams."—*Maidstone and Kentish Journal*.

" A very useful little adjunct this to the school-boy's geography."—*Kentish Observer*.

" This is a very useful school-book."—*Bath Express*.

" This little work gives the derivations of the names and terms occurring in the study of geography, and its contents are not only interesting but instructive. The etymology of various places, whose names are familiar to all, is given in a few words, clearly and concisely, and strike the reader at once as being admirably demonstrated. In a word, we consider this little work valuable both to student and teacher, and as such we cordially recommend it."—*Family Magazine*.

" The Author has produced a useful work for the rising generation, and one that will be found very acceptable to readers of maturer years………Appended to the work are important lists; constituting it altogether a valuable little book for reference."—*Lincoln, Rutland, and Stamford Mercury*.

" Will be found very useful to pupil-teachers and the ordinary scholars of our elementary schools, for whom it is chiefly designed; though information may be derived from it by all. There can be no question of the utility and importance of geographical nomenclatures. We have here a study of etymology, history, and geography blended... ......The book is entitled to general recognition. We cannot too strongly recommend it."—*Kentish Gazette*.

" ......The volume is filled with such derivatives, many of which are at once curious and instructive."—*London Journal*.

" There is some novelty in this class-book on geographical etymologies, and the lucid manner in which it is got up is creditable to the taste and judgment of the writer. A good deal of information is given in connection with the names of places."—*News of the World*.

" The purpose of Mr. Adams is 'to supply a list of geographical common and proper names arranged in such an order as to admit of easy reference.' We shall best illustrate the Author's meaning by the subjoined extract......A most useful little volume."—*Lloyd's Weekly Newspaper*.

." A publication of great interest, and will be found very useful in schools : we cannot think any system of geography complete that omits the explanation of the most important names and terms that occur in that science. A carefully prepared exposition of such proper names and technical terms, within a moderate compass, is supplied by Mr. Adams; and, whether as a class-book, or as a present for scholars, the book is a valuable addition to the school-room library."—*Essex Standard*.

" Mr. Adams has just published a very useful little work, entitled *The Geographical Word-Expositor*, containing correct explanations, descriptive and etymological, of terms and names occurring in the study of geography : it will be a great acquisition in all schools."— *Kent Herald*.

" The object of this pretty volume is to explain the terms occurring in the science of geography, etymologically and otherwise......So far as we remember, it is a new thing in the earth; the idea is an excellent one, and very excellently is it executed."—*British Banner*.

" Explains the meaning of many names, and proves the value of prefixes as well as affixes."—*Weekly Dispatch*.

" Within some hundred and fifty pages of a book which is almost capable of being carried in the waistcoat pocket, Mr. Adams compresses an explanation of the most important geographical common and proper names. As the alphabetical order is preserved, the enquirer has no difficulty in getting at the object of his search. The book will be found as useful out of schools as in them; for, though such knowledge adds a charm to the topic, scarcely a third even of well-educated persons are fully acquainted with the actual and literal meanings of many of the names of many places of the globe, and of the terms applying to them."—*Faversham Gazette*.

" *The Geographical Word-Expositor.*—Mr. Adams has issued a very useful and instructive little volume bearing the above title: it is intended more especially for the use of pupil-teachers and the upper classes in schools, but there are few who may not derive a considerable amount of information from the Author's research."—*Reading Mercury, and Oxford Gazette.*

" This is a cheap manual, designed for the use of pupil-teachers and schools, but will be found useful to all. The Author has adopted the dictum of Professor Sullivan, that, ' generally speaking, the names of places either indicate some peculiarity in their geographical position and character, or are commemorative of some occurrence or event in history.' The Author has bestown much labour in verifying the professor's proposition, and the result is a more useful and interesting little volume than would at first sight appear. It strikes us as being singularly accurate."—*Bell's News.*

" This unpretending little work is designed for the use of pupil-teachers and the upper classes in schools. It contains a large amount of information not often met with, and must facilitate the studies of those for whose use it is written."—*Little England's Illustrated Newspaper.*

" Destined to become extremely popular, supplying, as it does, a mass of information indispensable to all who desire to possess a knowledge of the circumstances which gave rise to the names of places, not only in our own country, but in all parts of the world......We have no hesitation in stating that the work conveys, in a pleasing and attractive form, more geographical and historical information than would be imparted to the mind of youth by the perusal of many a dry and lengthy treatise upon such subjects."—*Suffolk and Essex Free Press.*

" This very useful little volume is by the talented master of the Boys' Endowed National School, Dartford; and has been prepared especially for the use of teachers, pupil-teachers, and the upper classes in schools ; but should find a place also in every home. The great want long felt of a book on geographical nomenclatures adapted to the wants and capacities of youth is here supplied. It has been a work of great labour, but evidently a labour of love......We hope Mr. Adams will meet with encouragement in his valuable efforts to enlighten others, for he eminently deserves all that can be accorded to him."—*Dover Chronicle.*

" The second edition of Mr. Adams's *Geographical Word-Expositor* will no doubt be succeeded by a third and fourth : it contains just matter enough to show how the names of things become the names of places, and how the names of places find their way back sometimes into language as the names of things. The book tends to produce not only knowledge but thought, and deserves to be received thankfully into schools."—*Examiner.*

" We have great pleasure in calling the attention of parents, the heads of families, the principals of seminaries, and our readers generally, to the interesting little volume now before us, the Author of which has conferred a great benefit on the rising generation by its publication, inasmuch as not only children, but students of geography at a more advanced period of life, will find it a most useful auxiliary in their studies : it is an intelligible, concise, and important exposition of the terms employed in works on geography. Many of the names given to places in the five known divisions of the earth are extremely uncouth and apparently unintelligible, and hitherto, the students, in order to procure any information respecting them, have had to wade through many expensive works to obtain the knowledge of the true meaning or etymology of the word required. By the assistance of Mr. Adams's *Expositor* he is enabled to find it immediately. It has been not only highly approved of by a great number of our contemporaries in Great Britain and Ireland, but also by such eminent men as Dr. Latham, Mr. Edward Hughes (the celebrated geographer), the Rev. S. Clark, M.A., Principal of Battersea Training College, the Rev. Dr. Wilson, of the Royal College of Preceptors, and a great number of head masters of grammar and other schools. After such recommendations, equally creditable and honourable to the talents of the Author, any further commendation of this little work will be one of supererogation. Teachers of every grade will find it a most invaluable assistant in their geographical classes."—*Banbury Guardian.*

" This little book gives the meaning of geographical terms and names of places. It is designed for tyros in geography, who are not yet able to trace the meaning of the words from the learned or primitive languages from which they are derived. In teaching children geography, nothing can be more useful than to make them thoroughly acquainted with the terms used in the science, without a due knowledge of which they can never properly understand the subject. We have found this book particularly useful in this respect."—*Educational Times.*

" A very much needed help.......It is indeed a cleverly compiled little work, crowded with information. Mr. Adams has gathered, not without much painstaking, we are sure, a large amount of etymological lore."— *Sunday Teacher's Treasury.*

" A very useful school-book, well adapted for pupil-teachers and the upper forms of elementary schools."—*Gentleman's Magazine.*

" This is a dictionary of geographical terms, and a great deal more. The names and terms occurring in the science of geography are etymologically, scientifically, and historically explained. It contains information at once curious and useful, and in the highest degree valuable to the geographical student. Although professedly intended for the use of pupil-teachers and the upper classes in schools, it will be found available in a much wider circle. Persons who imagine that their education is complete will here find much that is new to them ; and to the large number who never cease self-education, this little book must be an indispensable manual. We add, for the benefit of our readers, that it is published at a price which places it within the reach of every one."—*Weekly Times.*

" This is an excellent little work of one hundred and sixty-six pages, well calculated to excite a deeper interest in geography : we cannot too highly recommend it to the heads of schools and families, and trust it will meet with the patronage it is so fairly entitled to."—*Market Rasen Weekly Mail.*

" This is indeed a very well written and useful work, and we most. cordially recommend it to every student. It reflects very great credit on the Author."—*Lincolnshire Free Press.*

" Mr. Adams's book is a most excellent one."—*Staffordshire Advertiser.*

" We had occasion, some little time since, to notice this valuable little work, and venture to predict for it a considerable share of popularity, which it seems to have speedily attained, a second edition having been called for within a few months. This edition, just issued, contains many important additions and improvements, including several useful appendices calculated to assist the student in attaining a thorough knowledge of what he reads. As a school-book, or as a volume of reference for 'children of a larger growth,' it will be found extremely valuable."—*Second Review of the Suffolk and Essex Free Press.*

"Useful and instructive.......Though small in bulk it contains a mass of information respecting the derivation of names, not only in our own country, but in all parts of the world."—*Family Herald.*

OPINIONS OF PRACTICAL EDUCATORS AND OTHERS.

"Your nice little book seems admirably adapted for the purpose for which it is intended; and I have no doubt that it wll meet with the circulation it so justly merits."—EDWARD HUGHES, Esq., F R.A S., F.R.G S., *Author of "Outlines of Physical Geography,"* etc.

"Well calculated to be useful."—REV. SAMUEL CLARK, M.A., F.R.G.S., *Principal of Battersea Training College, London,* etc.

"I have perused your *Expositor* with great pleasure. It is a very useful book, and I trust that you are meeting with the success which your performance deserves.—MONSIEUR A. HAVET, *Author of "The French Class Book."*

"A glance at these [contents] affords promise of considerable interest."—REV. W. H. BROOKFIELD, M.A., *one of H.M. Inspectors of Schools.*

"An excellent performance."—REV. DR. WILSON, F.C.P., etc.

"I think your book calculated to be extremely useful, and I have no doubt it will go very far to supply an existing want."—ALFRED BINGHAM, Esq., B.A., *Master of All Saints' School, Fulham.*

"You have touched a neglected string, and, I think, an important one. From a careful perusal of your work, I am sure that topography will receive a great assistance: and many, to whom the exposition of geographical terms and names was almost, if not entirely, unknown, will rejoice at perusing it, and hail with delight the important condensed information it contains. I heartily wish you success in the undertaking, and hope that it may speedily run through many editions and return you a rich reward for your labours."—ALFRED WILLIAM COLLINS, Esq., *Head Master, St Clement Danes Schools, London.*

"There has not yet fallen into my pupils' hands any book that has become such a favourite as your *Geographical Word-Expositor.* The more they use it, the more they like it."—JOHN H. HAY, Esq., *Author of " Hay's Class Register."*

" It will prove a valuable aid to teachers in the preparation of their geographical lessons. It will recommend itself not only for the amount of varied information it contains, but also as a key to geographical names in general."—GEORGE SYDENHAM, Esq., *Author of " Notes of Lessons in their principles and application."*

" Your excellent work needs only to become known to be duly appreciated. It supplies a gap in our geographical literature."—THOMAS CHALLENER, Esq., *Author of a " Catechism of the Descriptive Geography of England."*

" I feel no hesitation whatever in stating that your *Geographical Word-Expositor* will become one of our most valuable school-books."—JAMES CAMPKIN, Esq., *Author of the " Philosophy of Common Things."*

" Like most works produced by teachers, your valuable little book is thoroughly useful and practical."—JOHN JONES, Esq., *Author of " Notes of Lessons," and the " Liturgical Class-Book."*

" An excellent step.......I heartily wish your work a most extensive sale, and I shall do all in my power to bring it about."—P. H. HARDING, Esq., C.M., *Author of " Tabular Exercises in Arithmetic."*

" I cannot refrain from adding my testimony to the worth of your invaluable *Geographical Word-Expositor*."—HENRY D. BROOKE, Esq., *Author of " Text-Book of Arithmetic,"* etc.

" An *Expositor*, such as that which you have favoured the world with, has long been wanted, and numbers will, I think, feel grateful for the trouble you have taken for supplying that *desideratum*."—JOSEPH LONG, Esq., *Master of Stott Hill School, Bradford, Yorks.*

" I have much pleasure in recommending Mr. Adams's *Geographical Word-Expositor* to managers and teachers. It is, as far as I know, the only book of the kind in use among schools, and seems to be well calculated to promote the intelligent teaching of geography."—REV. WILLIAM CAMPBELL, M.A., *H.M. Inspector of Schools.*